TURNSKIN

TURNSKIN

STEVEN HAMMONDS

Rev. date: 10/10/2013

To order additional copies of this book, contact:
Xlibris LLC
0-800-056-3182
www.xlibrispublishing.co.uk
Orders@xlibrispublishing.co.uk
307429

CONTENTS

Chapter 1:   Run 7

Chapter 2:   Meeting.. 24

Chapter 3:   A Visit to the City.. 41

Chapter 4:   Investigation 51

Chapter 5:   Research Continues.. 65

Chapter 6:   A Stranger In The Village 75

Chapter 7:   Discovery.. 86

Chapter 8:   The Hunt 94

Chapter 9:   Escape 104

Chapter 10: Frenzy 117

Chapter 11: Return To England 131

Chapter 12: Sounds of the City.. 138

Chapter 13: Special Client 140

Chapter 14: Second Escape 148

Chapter 15: Recovery.. 156

Chapter 16: Release... 160

Chapter 17: Detective's Dilemma 163

Chapter 18: Retreat 167

Chapter 19: Life in the Forest 169

Chapter 20: Reunion... 175

Chapter 21: Something in the Woods................................ 179

Chapter 22: Confrontation... 185

Epilogue 187

Chapter 1

RUN

❦

DAN AWOKE SWEATING and tense, it had all seemed to real, all that killing and running, taking the woman by force and then being taken captive. It reminded him in parts of dreams he had as a child but this time it all seemed so real as if he had been there. He felt hungry so he rose from his bed, not bothering to put on a robe or turn any lights on. He walked quietly and nakedly to the refrigerator. Eagerly chewing on the half leg of lamb left over from Sunday lunch, then greedily gulping down several glasses of water. Earlier he had meant to re-cook the lamb as the centre had not thoroughly cooked and was still fairly pink, but this was now the meat he was eating and not the tough outer edges which if anything were overcooked (he thought absently he must have put the oven on to a high temperature again). As he swallowed the last few chunks of undercooked mean parts of his dream flashed disjointedly to him, a feeling of a time when the thought of meat anything other than still warm from its lifeblood and completely raw was all the sustenance he needed and craved.

Returning to his bed his companion, unaware of his leaving, stirred in the bed and he climbed back under the covers, quickly drifting into a dreamless sleep, or was it? Simply because he did not remember did not mean he did not dream at all.

He rose late, Beryl had gone; hastily dressing he rushed up the street to where he head left his old Ford. He always parked at the top of the hill because, if as usual it would not start, at least he could roll down the long hill and have a good chance of getting going. Every morning cursing and promising to work more hours and buy a better car with the extra money (he never did though). By the time he got the car going and made it through the city traffic he arrived at work an hour late. Grumbling and apologising for his time-keeping he went into the antique shop and bookstore in which he worked for what he felt was not enough money to survive on anywhere near as comfortably as he would like. But there was something endearing about old man Polanski who kept the shop, he never really complained about Dan's timekeeping. Young Dan was easy going and a good worker when he put his mind to it. He also had a kind ear to the old man's fabled stories and tales of times far distant to to-day's hustle and bustle of life.

An escape Dan relished and often wished he had been born in, a different time, would his life have been bettor or did he only dream of pastures greener. Then last night's dream came to him, they certainly didn't seem to be dreams of a better life and the more he thought on them the deeper his mood became. Old man Polanski noticed Dan brooding and pottering around the shop having to mention things two or three times before Dan would respond. Tiring of this he eventually sat Dan down in the back of the shop having just made a fresh pot of tea and tried to talk of what was on his mind.

Dan did not find it easy to talk about how much his dreams had bothered him and so tended to gloss over relating the tale in his dream and claimed he must just feel under the weather was probably the real reason for his mood. Polanski listened not commenting on the tales and told Dan to go home and get some rest. Dan went straight home, climbed into a hot bath and just relaxed soaking in the warm caress of the water. Drying off he called Beryl to ask if she would like to eat out for tea just for a change.

"But Dan, I thought I told you I was going straight out from work with the girls and staying at my parent's house tonight. Oh! got to go, the boss has just come into the office. See you in the week. Bye."

The phone went dead. Dan sat feeling glum and brooding over his troubled dreams. Damn her, why was it she always went out on the night he wanted to do something with her. "Right, if she can go out so can I, but who with?" Dan said. Dan dressed in jeans and a sweatshirt and a leather jacket. It was only six o'clock so it looked like what Beryl called an "early doors." First stop after a twenty minute walk was The Nag's Head, not the smartest pub in town but they kept a good beer. Dan sat alone at the bar enjoying the relaxing feeling as the third pint of strong real ale disappeared from his glass. Leaving the pub he strolled contentedly and fifteen minutes down the read found him outside the City Park Palm House, a pub and a restaurant on the perimeter of its namesake, The City Park. Once in the bar, a glass of strong lager with a large brandy chaser, he picked up both drinks and made his way into the restaurant area finding a small table on the far side of the room with patio windows overlooking the park. The menu was expensive but what the hell if he squandered what little he had saved for a new car. He felt strange, mixed up, he needed cheering up. The French onion soup merely made him realise just how hungry he was. He ordered a large carafe of red wine. Enjoying the warm infusion of alcohol on his nervous system, he felt less tense already. A large rump steak followed by crepes flambe in brandy. Finishing the wine and ordering several more large brandies, it was ten-twenty by the time he settled his bill and left the restaurant. Deciding to walk through the park, feeling very relaxed and contented, the dreams that had bothered him so much seemed unimportant now. Towards the centre of the park the street lights did little to illuminate the open patches of grass, let alone the wooded areas. The first he knew about his attackers was a feeling of someone coming up behind him, by the time he turned in his drunken state, it was too late. A large youth slammed into him knocking him to the ground, three bodies dropped on him laughing and shouting at how easy this one would be. Rage welled up inside Dan, his fingers instantly finding one of his assailant's throat, closing their grip then tearing back against the resistance of skin and tendons and finally feeling the hot flow of blood from the assailant's throat. Wriggling and squirming out from under one corpse and two startled youths Dan fled the scene keeping to the trees until he came to the edge of the park.

Trying to keep to the shadows he made his way home. Stripping off his bloodied clothes and showered. Confused and tired he fell into a troubled sleep, waking at early dawn with no plan in his mind other than to run and hide.

Picking up his passport and wallet he dressed in a pair of baseball boots, jeans, sweatshirt and teeshirt, all of which were old and comfortable. Dan put a few other things in a bag, picked up his sheepskin flying jacket and went up the hill to his Ford. Luckily it started quite easily. He headed out toward the city stopping at the cash dispenser. Putting in his card and typing out his number code, the machine informed him that he had £13.76 available for withdrawal in denominations of £10 only. He took £10. "A long way that will get me" he said sarcastically, "and as for this car do I give myself up, what chance have I got?" Returning to his car a thought struck him, old man Polinski's car was almost new, well only three or four years old, and who would think of looking for a Lada as a getaway car? He drove across the city parking his Ford in a multistorey car park about a mile away from Polanski's shop. The old man lived above in a tiny flat which he claimed was all he needed. Fifteen minutes later Dan was outside the shop and Polanski's car was in a space ten yards around the corner in a side street. Polanski had always trusted Dan with a set of keys for the shop and Dan knew that he kept a spare set of car keys on top of the safe in the back room. Quietly Dan opened the front door reaching for the bell trigger and silencing it just before it triggered the bell. Carefully making his way into the back room he found the keys and out of curiosity he gave the handle on the safe a pull; it opened. Old man Polanski had a habit of forgetting to lock it on occasions. Dan lifted out the cash box, it was locked but it did not feel empty, a little change rattled but not too loudly, it was muffled by paper. Hastily Dan left the shop, carefully closing the front door but not locking it. He rounded the corner to Polanski's Lada. Opening the car he put his bag on the back seat and the cash box on the floor deciding to wait before he opened it. People were beginning to appear on their way to work for the day. Dan started up the Lada and drove South out of the city hoping to be clear before the morning traffic jams started.

Twenty miles from Dover he pulled in at a Happy Eater which had a few customers for early breakfast. Parking away from the other cars in the car park he got out and took a small tool kit from the boot of the car. Using a screwdriver and a bit of effort he managed to pry the cash box open. He was shocked. What was the old man doing with £827 and odd pence in his cash box? Still mine in not to reason why just be grateful for such luck he thought. Now he could formulate a plan, he could at least afford to get abroad. Starting up the Lada he drove out into the traffic heading straight for Dover, his first idea being to get onto a ferry.

Arriving at the ferry terminal Dan parked up and checked the time of departing ferries, it was now ten thirty, there was a Dover to Zebrugge leaving at eleven. He went to the booking office and purchased a ticket on way, worried that he had to give the car's registration number to the clerk but it was too late to change the plates on the car. Let's face it Dan (he thought to himself) this isn't going to be the last risk you take, is it? By eleven fifteen he felt a little easier. Sitting in the bar as the ferry was under way to Zebrugge the hot coffee even if a little bitter helped ease his tension as he tried to think of what next. One step at a time, he felt just getting through Passport Control was worrying enough, although there was no reason for him to be suspected on his crimes so soon, expect maybe the car, but that isn't exactly a matter for Interpol. "Lada thief stopped on ferry", he thought, "so ridiculous it would probably make the headlines." Stop it, this isn't helping realising he hadn't just thought it but said it aloud. A couple on the next table looked up from their meal and stared at him as if he were a simpleton. When his eyes met theirs they turned their attention back to their meals and muttered quietly to each other. Dan finished his coffee and went for a walk around the boat taking deep breaths of salty air trying to relax. Just pretend you're on your holiday he thought stopping half way through the sentence to make sure he was only thinking it and not talking it again. It didn't seem too long until the ferry was docking and Dan was driving off the ferry through the customs area. He wasn't even stopped, that was a relief. But now where? he thought, if he was to head into East Germany, with the wall coming down a few years ago, surely passport control would not be so rigorous and then where? Oh well! one step at a time. But then he didn't even have a map, he couldn't speak any language other than English. God, why don't I ever get things right. Feeling despondent and very disconsolate Dan found himself a small shop, what he would call a supermarket (what they would call it he didn't care) and bought some wine, bread and cheese relieved that

they accepted his English currency. Getting back into the car Dan was
irritable his nerves were on edge. He drove. No definite direction, just
head inland who fucking cares. "Christ, what's happening to me" he
was talking to himself again aloud. "Ah sod it, who is going to hear me
now anyway." Dan didn't have any idea where he was heading it was
late evening and he was in a built-up area. He was tired but he didn't
want to rest until he was at least in the countryside.

Although Dan was getting tired he kept on driving. Stopping
only to refuel he did not otherwise stop until the sun had long set.
He had no particular idea where he was going but something inside
made him stay heading East. He had passed a sign saying Dusseldorf
and though maybe he could find a hotel but fear of being found
made him hesitate before anything positive had started to form in
his mind. "What am I going to do?" he was talking to himself again.
A horn blared and lights dazzled him startling him to his senses. He
swerved back to the right side of the road just in time to avoid the
oncoming ruck. "You idiot, that was too close for comfort. Good
job you went the right way. Will you get some rest." He really was
holding conversations with himself now. Starting to feel as if he was
going to crack up completely Dan pulled the car off the road into a
lay-by, turned off the lights and locked all the car doors. He reached
over to the half empty bottle of wine. Uncorking it and taking a good
swallow he reached for the last of the bread and cheese and sated
his hunger mechanically, not really tasting anything. His head was
spinning "How did this happen?"—talking to himself again. He took
another couple of swallows of wine, re-corked the bottle putting it
back on the passenger seat. Dan sat back in the none too comfortable
driver's seat and had drifted into a fitful sleep within seconds. His
dreams were vivid though disjointed, one minute he was home with
friends drinking, the next he was in a wilderness with hot breath on

his neck making him run to get away, stumbling over fields, then, just as suddenly as it started it changed to him sitting in a restaurant eating. No being eaten, but both diner and meal had his face. He woke with a start, it was cold, he reached into the back of the car for his jacket. Pulling the sheepskin collar up around his neck he rubbed his legs vigorously then sat back closing his eyes again, hoping the visions of his dreams would fade with once again trying to relax. Relax, he could not, he thought to drink the last of the wine then changed his mind, all he needed was to get stopped for drinking by the police even if he wasn't actually driving the car at the time, who knows what might happen and he wasn't too sure of the rules and regulations concerning foreign police procedures. He wasn't even sure that he might not get pulled for sleeping in the car. He was still sitting numbly wondering about the strangeness of the predicament when the sun started to creep into the sky.

Dan started driving again with the dawn, hoping to find his way through Dresden and on Eastward before the morning traffic. Two hours later he found his way out and without having any idea how he had managed to get through and still be heading in the right direction. "What is the right direction looney when you don't know where it is you're going. Oops! there you go again talking to yourself." He didn't chide himself anyway he then thought if he was going to talk to himself he might as well enjoy the company. Dan had always felt that he was lucky when it came to a sense of direction. He had driven over most of England having never used a map, although he thought it might be a good idea to get one now, but decided to just carry on for now following the sun as it crept higher. Stick to the golden rule, he thought. When in doubt go straight on. A little while later he decided to stop to rest and eat. He pulled over at a place called Biedenkiopf. He found a shop with a storekeeper who fortunately spoke a little English and managed to buy some bread, cooked sausage, cheese and several bottle of spring water. He also bought a map book, even if it was written in German, at least it might give him an idea on which way to go. The shopkeeper also changed a little of his sterling for Deuchmarks. Dan felt a little easier about stopping for the likes of petrol and then later on maybe he could find a cheap hotel. But come to that in good time. Returning to the car Dan ate a little breakfast while studying the map he had bought. Best to stay off the main routes, he thought, there may be toll roads, I know they have them in France so probably they have them here too. He worked out where he was and then set a basic route, again heading East and set off for the rest of the day determined to make good distance. The only thing that would ease his nerves he thought. By the time midnight approached having only stopped once for a brief rest and to refuel, he was coming to the outskirts of Dresden. "Surely I could make better time if I used the main roads." He felt downhearted again and his anxiety was turning into depression as he pulled over again wondering if it would be safe to try a hotel for the night.

Starting up a few minutes later he drove on, eventually finding what looked like a small hotel with a bar, though he had no idea whether it would be open at this time of night. Parking the car off the road he walked up to he door and pushed it, it was locked and just rattled to his pressure. He was just about to turn away when it opened and a large portly man stood in his shirt sleeves, balding and smelling of garlic, he spoke to Dan. Dan didn't understand a word then tried to gesture and after a minute or two of disjointed speech decided to give up. At that moment a small stony faced, grey haired woman said something sharp to the big balding man and he stepped aside taking Dan gently by the arm. Dan's mind raced, should he strike out, or flee? The big German looked like he would laugh at Dan's shot. His heart was pounding, a thousand things raced through his mind, the fight in the park, the dreams of being hunted and of really being hunted. Almost instantly the tension broke, the old lady spoke in a heavily accented mix of German and English.

"You need somewhere to stay for the night? Mein Herr."

Dan's reply was no clearer, he stuttered "Just a room for the night, if you please. Thanks."

"Come in Mein Herr, you take no mind of mine husband", she paused before adding "Him drunkard anywise. I've got a nice room for you, follow please."

She led Dan up an old staircase and opened a door on the first landing, he followed her into a small but cosy bedroom with a single bed, wardrobe and washstand, other than a single dining chair against the wall that was it. Dan took out his money and asked "How much?" but the old lady waved her hand and said "No, in tomorrow morning we settle, you look tired now."

Closing the door behind the old lady Dan lay back on the bed, pulled off his trainers and sighed, realising just how tired he was. After about three minutes he was about to get up, have a wash and undress. There was a knock at the door. Dan eased the door open and there was the big bald German smiling at him through glazed eyes. He was holding a tray with a plate of sandwiches and a large bottle of beer on it. These he pushed at Dan, turned and strode away before Dan could say anything. He closed the door and laid the try on the bed, pulled up the chair. The sandwiches were a kind of salami and washed down nicely with the cold beer.

Dan woke with sunlight coming through the window. He washed, dressed and headed downstairs. The little old lady was cleaning around the bar area and bid him "Gooden morgan, Mein Herr, I hope you sleep well, Yar?"

"Thank you, I did." Dan said although it wasn't strictly true, he had been restless all night troubled by fears and bad dreams. "May I pay you now please?" Dan asked, talking fairly slowly but not too slow as to offend the starched but pleasant old lady. The bill was settled and Dan thanked her again. Relieved as he left that he had the forethought to use Bill Smith as his name on the register, a formality he had hoped to avoid. He had already used the name of Dave Tarrant at the shop where he had changed his cash. "Just for the receipt" the cashier had said.

Still just keep track of which name and who you tell it to he thought to himself. Better refreshed than from his previous night, Dan set off determined to keep moving all day. By lunchtime he was across the border into Poland. Although there was little fuss that he had no papers for the car, it had cost him his watch and more than a few heartbeats. The watch had been a birthday present from Beryl and quite an expensive one at that, but he was through the border now.

"No point crying over its loss" again the talking had started, it seemed to happen when he was most nervous. He pressed on trying hard to relax and take in the wonderful countryside, after all summer was just around the corner. Dan kept trying to pretend he was just on holiday. He was approaching the city of Krakov when he remembered the old man Polanski had talked of the beauty of the old city of kings. "Well, maybe I could do the tourist bit, I need to relax if only to stop talking to myself." He remembered bits and pieces of what old man Polanski had told him. Not far from the Tatra and Carpathian mountains, a mediaeval city, surely at this time of year Dan could blend into the city's tourists, coming and going without being noticed too much. Only one way to find out he thought. He parked the car in a quiet space with a few other cars parked about, wanting it to be as inconspicuous as possible but also easy to find his way back to. Making a mental note of his surroundings he locked his bag and sheepskin coat in the boot of the car keeping his wallet and passport with him. Wandering around taking in the charm of the city he stopped for a drink at a small roadside cafe and just about managed to converse in gestures and pointing with a little mime thrown in for good measure. The locals seemed to find him quite amusing. Dan wandered around a little on edge but trying to relax taking in the sights of impressive and historic architecture and monuments. As the sun began to set he decided to make his way back to the car, stopping for one more drink on the way. The place he stopped in was fairly busy, it seemed a multitude of different languages going all at once. Tourists, Dan thought as he looked around at what he could only describe as an old world tavern. A group of Germans about six or seven in all were noisily swilling beer much to the chagrin of the owner. He sauntered over, a tall lean man with white hair and a hooked nose, saying something to Dan in a deep voice, a little louder than was necessary for Dan to hear, whereupon quite a few heads turned to stare. Dan wishing he could have just crawled into a hole and hid, fumbled quickly for his wallet, taking out the wad of English money he had taken from old man Polanski's safe stuttering "It's OK, I can ppay, will you accept English money?" The innkeeper took a ten pound note off Dan, grunted something at him and signalled to the waiter to give him his beer. Walking back to the bar and his cronies, they all seemed preoccupied in examining the note. Not long afterwards the waitress approached Dan again, Oh! what now he thought, but she simply handed him the try with his change on it. He picked up most of it leaving a little for a tip, not having any idea what any of it was worth, he hoped it was enough not to offend.

As she turned to walk away she said very quietly in an accent he could just about grasp "You English, careful watch" then made her way around the room clearing up the odd table here and there. Dan finished off the last of his beer and thought it easier to leave than anything like that performance again. He was wound up enough not to need this kind of aggrievation as well.

The streets were quite busy as Dan retraced his steps back towards where he had left the car. He thought to stop for something to eat but he was on edge and didn't want another public exhibition. Turning into the street where he had left the car something slammed into him from behind knocking him to the floor. He tried to struggle to his feet when he was knocked down again, rolling on to his back he caught a glimpse of half a dozen men as two started kicking at him and two more tried to pin him down while the other two were trying to rifle his pockets. It was the group of rowdy Germans from the tavern. Dan wriggled and struggled to get free but the kicks were slamming into his stomach and back, he had to do something soon or he would pass out. Twisting and kicking out himself he managed to cause one of his assailants to stumble while another lost his grip. Then as one of his attackers who was trying to get at his pockets came within reach Dan automatically lashed out and caught him by the throat. His fingers tightened and began to close. A memory flashed through his mind of the attack in the park. Suddenly his attackers were scattering and running except the one he had hold of. Dan looked into his assailant's eyes, they were bulging with tears being squeezed out of the swollen, crimson tear ducts. Then suddenly Dan was knocked out senseless by something hard. His head spun down into a dark hazy gloom, the last thing he remembered was a policeman bending over him.

Dan came to in the back of a bouncing van with a policeman sitting next to him. It was a short ride to the police station where he was roughly bundled out. Two men read something to him, none of which he could understand, what did confuse him was why he was alone. When the police had come why had they not caught his attackers.

"This is all back to front" Dan complained, but they just shushed him and made him empty his pockets. He put the car keys and change the waitress had given him on the desk then reached into his back pocket for his wallet and passport. He gave over his passport but his wallet had gone. He complained and gestured but it did no good, none of the officers present could speak a word of English. Two of the policemen then frisked him and led him to a cell, a solid steel door with a shutter in it, the ring seemed to resonate for minutes as the door slammed shut. Alone in this tiny cell Dan sat on the steel cot wincing from the pain in his ribs.

Thoughts of being sent home to face a murder charge reeled in his mind. "Why me" he cried, "why me." Dan lay back on the cot trying to stifle the sobs he could not control any longer, all of the stress he thought he had controlled so far was coming to the surface. He squeezed his eyes tightly shut trying to close out the world knowing inside it wasn't going to go anywhere tonight. He thought, maybe they don't know anything about me here and will let me go, but he wasn't exactly confident of that, not the way his luck had been going lately.

He tried to think of home and Beryl and wished he could turn back time and that he had been more understanding towards her.

Early next morning Dan was woken by a policeman who took him to a room with two other men waiting in it, one man was in uniform and the other wore a suit. The uniformed man spoke in Polish then the man in the suit said in broken English "You are Daniel Hunter?" he waited for Dan's answer. "Erm, yes sir."

"You were arrested last night for fighting." Dan was confused and scared not knowing if they knew about him. "I, I was defending myself. I was attacked by half a dozen German thugs, they stole my wallet and my money, didn't you arrest any of them?"

The man in the suit spoke in Polish to the other officer then turned and spoke to Dan again. "You were arrested last night for fighting, no others were arrested. We will look into this, but for now" he paused and spoke again to the officer then asked Dan where he was staying.

"I don't have anywhere yet, I'd only just arrived when this happened." Dan couldn't keep the nervousness out of his voice.

The man in the suit wrote something down on a paid and said "You will go and book in here" he handed the note to Dan "You stay there and tomorrow you will return here to see the judge. We will have more information of what happened then." With that the man in uniform handed Dan an envelope, in it was his change and car keys but no passport. Dan asked for it "You will get it back tomorrow when you have seen the judge and we have checked things out.

It took Dan over an hour to find the car, his mind was reeling "What now!" he was openly talking to himself whilst walking in the street. He opened the car door and sat in the driver's seat hunching the steering wheel and shouting "What now, Well come on what." Taking a deep breath he tried to calm himself. Dan thought, if they decide to check up on him he's had it. He couldn't believe his luck when they had let him out on his own recognisance trusting him to come back, but then, who understands the way the police work, maybe they had him followed but no, what for.

He was confused, should he go to the address the policeman had given him, maybe they might get his money back. "Some chance!" He was talking to himself again "But where can I go, they've got my passport."

He started the car, the mountains he thought, cross the mountains. I've got to find something, my luck has got to change. Eventually finding his way out of Krakov, this time he headed South, or at least what he thought was South. After a while he saw a sign for Zakopane and the Czechoslovakian border. Realising he couldn't cross the border without his passport he turned off at a narrow road just passed somewhere called Nowtarg the road twisted and turned winding into the hills.

"Oh Christ no, this is all I need" Dan didn't even realise he was talking aloud again "Don't do this to me." The car was starting to overheat, he pulled over to the edge of the road. "If anyone wants to get past it's tough."

Dan got out and went to the front of the car. Opening the bonnet he resisted the temptation to unscrew the radiator cap "No let it cool down first." He walked round to the boot of the car to get out a bottle of the mineral water he had bought. He touched the boot lid, it came open without him unlocking it. "Oh Jesus, it's been forced. When!" His jacket and bag had gone, fortunately one of the bottles of water was still there next to the simple tool kit old man Polanski kept.

Dan was dazed things were just not working out for him. He picked up the bottle of water and took it round to the front of the car and sat on the ground waiting for the radiator to cool.

Fifteen minutes later he slowly unscrewed the radiator cap and poured the water in keeping the empty bottle. He started up the Lada and drove on keeping a watchful eye on the temperature gauge.

After a few more miles he spotted a mountain stream just ten yards from the road, he pulled over. It took three trips to fill the radiator and refilling the bottle for a fourth time he set off again.

After a long while he passed through a small village the like of which he never dreamed would exist in this day and age. He pressed on although the road was getting considerably rougher as he went on, it was also getting even steeper and Dan was feeling considerably fraught and worried. After another three quarters of an hour up the climb Dan rounded a sharp bend the there it was right out of a mediaeval story book.

The castle was grand and imposing, he wouldn't have stopped but the road led to nowhere else, the gates were open so he drove straight in the courtyard. "What happens now, Oh Jeez here comes Drac."

Dan climbed out of the car as the man came out of the main door and started towards him. He was dressed in butler's livery, he approached Dan and stopped saying something in Polish that Dan could not understand at all.

"I am English, I am sorry to trouble you, I've been having trouble with my car."

The butler simply looked at Dan and said "Come in Sir."

Dan followed him into the castle and the butler showed Dan into a large hallway then through a door, then into another large room filled with furniture which looked antique and entirely in keeping with the outward appearance of the castle. An antique dealer's dream come true this place was the first thing Dan thought as he walked into the room.

"Vait here" was all the butler said as he turned and left Dan alone in what was the first castle reception room Dan had ever seen, let alone been in.

Chapter 2

MEETING

⚜

"WELCOME TO MY home, I believe you are English", he didn't give Dan time to answer although Dan did hesitate, he had used several different names and he was beginning to forget which one he used last. "Erm, yes I am Dan Gale, and you are?"

Forgive me I should have introduced myself. First I am Count Manfred Versipellis, the thirtieth direct descendant of the first count of Karpaty."

"I'm sorry I didn't mean to appear rude, it's just I've been on the road so long, I'm tired and it's been so long since I've talked to someone who speaks such good English."

"Time a plenty to talk, first rest and wash, Mishcow will show you to your room, you will find clean clothes in the wardrobe, some should fit, there are plenty all of my own, please indulge yourself."

Dan let it all wash over him thinking this is like a fifties black and white movie. Thanking the count and following Mishcow up two spiralling flights of stairs he entered a room with a solid wood panelled door leading to a large ornate room of what must be thirty feet square with a window leading to an ornate veranda overlooking the central courtyard of the castle. The room itself was fantastic.

Beautiful inlaid wardrobes covered the entire length of one wall, while its facia wall was completely mirrored, very old faded mirrors which seemed to distort your reflection in a strange way not like you would expect a fairground mirror to show but not an ordinary mirror either. Dan merely put it down to his tiredness and the fading light.

The wall with the door was hung with tapestries depicting what Dan saw as a mediaeval foxhunt but with a man figure in amidst the hounds and the quarry was too indistinct to say what it was.

An enormous four poster bed sat almost central in the room and as soon as Mishcow had excused himself Dan collapsed onto it and slept heavily for what felt like years.

Gently, Mishcow awakened him intimating that he should follow him. Dan did so across the hall, there was a hot bath and towels waiting. Mishcow left him saying something, Dan had no comprehension of what. He undressed and bathed feeling the warmth of the water soak through him relishing the feeling that for the first time in days he could stop worrying what was behind him.

Wrapping himself in a large soft towel he crossed the hall to his room where he found Mishcow laying out some clothes for him. As soon as he entered the room Mishcow graciously acknowledged his presence, bowed and left him to dress saying in very poor English "deener in sirty minut, sank you" quietly closing the door behind him.

The clothes Mishcow had laid out for him were surprisingly a good fit. He had noticed he had lost a little weight whilst on the run. Even when dressed he felt like someone out of the cast of War and Peace. Calf length leather boots, a little tight but of such soft leather not to be uncomfortable, no underwear but grey breeches close fitting of a silken type of cloth soft against the skin, a coarse cotton shirt and light cotton jacket. Dan couldn't help thinking with a laugh a 17th century bomber jacket in red.

A gong sounded and suddenly the thought of a hot cooked meal came to him. Leaving the room and retracing his way down to the ground floor Dan found Mishcow who then led him to the dining room.

"Good evening Mr Gale" Count Versepillis said rising as Dan entered the room. "Let me introduce you to my sister Anastasia."

Dan noticed the slim dark haired girl with high cheekbones and a very pale complexion. She nodded graciously but said nothing, Dan acknowledged her bidding her good evening.

"Sit and we shall eat, come make yourself at home, Mr Gale."

"Please call me Dan and let me say I am grateful to you for your hospitality." Dan took a sofa opposite Annastasia sitting down under the gaze of the Count at the head of the table.

"I trust you rested well", the Count was certainly very hospitable although Dan felt uneasy in these surroundings. The dining hall was huge with massive log fires at either end, each must have taken half a tree to fill the grate. More tapestries hung from the torch lit walls depicting more hunting scenes and battles. Dan complimented the Count on the grandeur of the castle and its decor feeling it only polite for him to make an effort at conversation.

The food served was plain, but good, a vegetable soup to start followed by a steak of something, though definitely not beef (Dan thought it indiscreet to ask what) served with plain vegetables followed by a selection of cheeses with bread and biscuits. All through the meal Mishcow never let Dan's wine glass become empty.

"You are so secluded here does it not get to you?" As soon as Dan said it he though oh God, manners and grammar, think idiot, then he immediately apologised for such a rude question.

"There is no need to apologise, no offence is taken, it is perfectly understandable for you to be curious. My family have been here for more than thirty generations.

My ancestors settled here in the mid nine hundreds when they moved from Krakow in 969 when the first bishopric of Krakow was formed. Latin and Orthodox faith were established in the area by this time. My ancestor, a great fighting and hunting man, felt constricted by the religious movement and to be honest a little threatened, so whilst openly declaring devotion to Miesko the First he moved his home and family to the Carpathians on some pretext of family matters and began the building of this castle here today, though much of it has changed and been rebuilt over the centuries, some of it, such as its sub-structure still remains the same. His real reason for seeking out this recluse was he secretly did not approve or believe in the impending growth of religion but realised the futility of trying to stand against it.

You see Count Stanislaw Oliwa Versipellis was an alchemist, frowned upon by those of godly beliefs. His beliefs and habits were a well-kept secret so no one suspected anything other than the reasons he declared for moving into seclusion. For he was a great alchemist and would surely be branded a heretic if the truth ever were to be found out."

The Count appeared in his element whilst telling his tale though Dan was genuinely impressed commenting that.

"I have always thought of myself as an athiest despite being a Protestant, still people are more understanding towards non-believers these days, don't you think?"

"Ah, but it was not just a case of not believing" added the Count. "Stanislaw's level of alchemy is almost a religion in itself, do you not think?"

"I had no idea of the theories or uses of alchemy, I merely thought it an early form of chemistry, Count" Dan was saying as Mishcow once again refilled his glass. "Surely modern science has long overtaken those old beliefs and uses of whatever it was they used in old times although I must admit my knowledge of such things is nothing more than an old man's tales. It's not a subject I've really given much thought to."

"Yes, but Mr Gale."

"Call me Dan please Count."

"Very well, Dan, as I was saying, your viewpoint is that which I would expect you see with the coming of the great religions. Most secrets of old science were lost to most men, only those who chose to continue their practices had to do so in great secrecy. But today the blend of the old science and the new has made our art a formidable power, in a scientific manner, of course."

"Count, you say 'our art' as if you still practice it?" Dan questioned him and then wished he had not.

"I merely state what has been in my family for generations as ours as in our heritage, Mr Gale."

Dan could not miss the tightness in the Count's voice and the look in those cold eyes. "Ah! but you must be tired Dan." Instantly it was as if the Count had changed into another personality again once more congenial but still a little guarded.

"Forgive me, there will be time a plenty for us to talk tomorrow, as for tonight, I trust you will rest well. Please treat my home as if it were your own."

"You are most kind Count, yes I am a little tired. I thank you for your kind hospitality and look forward to tomorrow. Now I shall bid you and your gracious sister good night."

With that Dan was shown to his room by Mishcow who removed the bedwarmer in Dan's bed and laid out a flannel nightshirt for Dan. With a small nod Mishcow left Dan in the candlelight room with not a word, closing the door gently. Dan was already half undressed by the time the door closed and soon after, dressed only in the nightshirt climbed into the large four poster and after putting out the last of the candles he soon drifted into a deep relaxed sleep.

Dan awoke, his head was thumping, the morning sun was streaming into his room from gaps in the curtains. Sitting up he saw his own clothes cleaned and laid out for him. Rising sluggishly he crossed the hall to the bathroom and made the best effort he could to refresh himself. God, how much wine did I drink last night, he thought.

Returning to his room he dressed and pulled open the curtains. Opening the door he stood on the veranda taking in deep breaths in an effort to put some fresh oxygen into his blood stream, hoping that with it his head might not feel quite as bad as it did.

It was then he heard a chilling scream from somewhere distant in the castle, the hair on the back of his neck stood on end and he shivered wondering what it could be.

That instantly brought him back to the memory of all that had happened in the last few days. His nerves right on edge he wondered how much longer he would keep his sanity for he could not go on like this.

"Good morning Dan", the Count was calling him from a doorway in the courtyard. "Will you join me for a ride in the country before breakfast?"

"But I have never ridden a horse" relied Dan, presuming that was what the Count meant more from the boots and jodhpurs he was wearing than any other reason.

"That is not a problem, by the time we return you will be able to, I have the perfect horse for you. A mare, she is so docile all you will have to do is sit on her back and she will do the rest."

Dan was tempted, "OK I'll be right down." The Count seemed to have a talent for putting Dan at ease so very quickly.

By the time Dan found his way to the courtyard the Count had the two mounts waiting. A large grey stallion with a beautiful ornate saddle etched with what Dan presumed was the Count's heraldic emblem. Dan mounted a small by mare standing passively untethered as if in awe of the grey.

The Count showed Dan how to mount his horse then almost vaulted into the saddle of the grey, he instantly kicked his horse to a trot towards the arched gates of the castle. Dan's simply followed the grey as if she were being towed behind.

The Count was a picture of elegance, his tall slender but powerful frame and flowing greyish hair looking as if he were tailor made to sit upon such a graceful animal; a sharp contrast to Dan, shorter and wirey in an old sweatshirt and jeans, with his close cut hair he felt like all last night's wine was being churned inside him; but soon his white knuckle grip on the reins relaxed and he began to settle into a more comfortable rhythm which improved by virtue of more advice from the Count.

The countryside was startlingly beautiful; passing through a valley they left the old rocky road which led from the village to the castle and crossed into lush grassy hills and gullies, crossing many small streams and passing woods, some sparse looking as if wood had been cut freshly from the land, but others dense barely penetrable by man and horse.

"There is great hunting in the mountains here" the Count was shouting over his shoulder. "The venison you ate last night I brought down not far from here myself."

Dan was working hard on staying in the saddle and a little out of breath to answer back.

Whilst passing one of the more densely forested slopes Dan raggedly gathered his breath and shouted to the Count "Would you mind if we rested a while, please."

Slowing to a walk the Count turned to Dan and gave a hearty laugh. "Ha, ha, tiring already Dan, yes we will rest soon, but not here, these woods are a little dangerous and we don't carry any arms with us except for my hunting knives. Let's head over this way into cleaner ground."

Whereupon the Count turned the grey and kicked into a trot, Dan's mare obediently following along.

Another ten minutes riding brought them to a stream meandering through open ground covered in rocky outcrops, grassy areas spotted with wild flowers, they came to a half letting the horses drink from the stream.

Dan dismounted, complaining "Jeezus, you might have warned me, the seams of these jeans are cutting my thighs in two."

The Count just laughed and said "I'll have one of the servant girls rub them with some salve for you when we return, OK."

Dan said "Well, maybe it was worth having sore legs after all", then they both sat in the grass laughing. The Count passed Dan a flask, taking a gulp from it Dan wheezed "Wow! what is that."

"Just a blend of herbs and a little alcohol, it will help get your blood circulating."

Dan passed the flask back to the Count and cautiously mentioned the scream he had heard this morning. The Count seemed to look through Dan saying "Ah, probably one of the kitchen girls saw a mouse, a might too skittish to live in the mountains some of them."

"Talking of skittish" Dan replied, "Dare I say without offending you Count, but you seemed a trifle concerned about resting near the woods back there."

"Skittish is one thing, I am not afraid Dan. Cautious is one thing I am. Those woods can be dangerous, there are many wild animals in the mountains, most living in the seclusion and cover of thick woodlands. The hunting is good here but you must be prepared for many dangers in the thicket and woods. To-day we are not so prepared, so it's far safer to keep to the open country. And that my friend is by daylight. Under no circumstances should you wander in open country by night. The villagers lock themselves in their homes by dusk but they are a superstitious lot. Still it doesn't do to be rash in these parts.

"What king of superstitions do they have Count? I have heard many tales of European folklore from a man I used to work for. He told me many stories but I thought all that stuff was supposed to take place an Transylvania. You don't believe them do you?"

"Dan there are many things man cannot explain, most times it is easier to put them out of your thoughts. That does not mean they don't exist. Our local villagers sincerely believe in such creatures as vampires and werewolves, they believe that when a werewolf dies it can become a vampire. This I do not believe, but there are phenomena which cannot be explained happening in these mountains. Deer and even the odd bear have been found killed and mutilated. Now what animal could bring down a bear? Those woods are dangerous at night, be warned."

The Count's tone scared Dan, he felt a tingle run down and then physically shivered.

"Well, shall we head back to the castle," Dan asked, trying to keep the wavers out of his voice.

"Yes, Dan, let's go and eat breakfast."

Upon their return Dan ate an enormous breakfast of bacon, liver, kidneys, eggs and bread. Bloated and satisfied he let out a great sigh.

"I thank you for your hospitality Count, but I fear I must be moving on."

"Dan, my friend, I don't wish to pry but how do you intend to travel, have you not lost all your belongings other than the car. I could take you to the local police station if you wish but somehow I get the feeling that that's not somewhere you would feel comfortable."

Dan stuttered and before he could get out the words the Count asked directly. "What is it you run from my friend? If you would allow me I may be able to help you."

Dan didn't know were to start.

"Come Dan, we all make mistakes sometimes it helps to talk on them."

Through the rest of the day Dan poured out his heart and troubles to this mysterious stranger whom he had come to trust so quickly. By the time he had finished his sorry tale he was beginning to feel it less of a burden on his conscience. Maybe he should have stayed in England to face his fate, but it was too late for that now.

"Dan, I have work here you could help me with if you wish to stay on as my guest. We can easily dispose of your car and cover your tracks. besides this castle has a million places to hide in. You are welcome here as a friend Dan, please consider it."

It took Dan about ten seconds to consider it, besides what options did he have.

"I would be honoured to stay with you Count, only on the condition that I may earn my keep. I would be willing to work at anything with you if you think I can help."

"Very well, Mr Hunter, that is settled then let's have a drink to seal our contract and I'll tell you about the nature of my work here."

In sealing the contract there was very little talk of work but a lot of drinking. Dan felt as if he could begin to live all over again and that was to be celebrated. He eventually passed out drunk and didn't wake till late evening.

That evening as Dan stood on the veranda of his room looking out above the castle rooftops he could see noting but a heavy clinging mist although his thoughts were on the unseen mountains. old man Polanski had told him tales of creatures that lurk in darkness, living off the flesh of others, feared by the people, shunned by other wild animals except for those who profit from the beasts actions. Folk tales but surely not possible in the twentieth century.

Mishcow interrupted Dan's thoughts. "Dinner, Sir." It was only the second time he had spoken to Dan in English.

Doing his best not to show how much he had been startled, Dan thanked Mishcow and followed him down to the dining room.

"Good evening Dan." the Count greeted.

Returning the greeting to the Count and to his sister, Dan sat and was then surprised as she spoke freely for the first time since they had met.

"So you are joining our little family here Dan, and welcome to you."

"The pleasure is all mine, my lady."

"Please Dan, call me Anastasia, my stuffy brother may like to be addressed by his title but then who wouldn't with a name like Manfred. Though I shouldn't mock him he loves me dearly really."

"Anastasia does have a point Dan, I don't like my name too much and I find being called Count does give me a certain satisfaction."

Dan felt much more relaxed, especially with Anastasia's more open mood.

"I suppose", Anastasia spoke softly. "You wonder that we both are so fluent in your native tongue?"

"It did cross my mind." Dan replied.

"We were both educated in England. At fourteen I was placed in a Swiss finishing school, while Manfred studied Chemistry at London changing mid-course to medical college. You are in for hard labour if you are going to assist him in his work. I just hope you are not squeamish."

"Enough Anna, we are about to eat, there is time aplenty to introduce Dan to my work. Suffice to say your interest in folklore stories will be to your benefit in accepting some of my findings. Now no more, let's eat."

The Count was adamant and it was obvious he would let Dan know of his work in his own time, and no other way. The conversation turned to the more cheerful subject of Anastasia.

Though not pretty Dan was beginning to find her beguiling in her own way. A sweet young lady with a pleasant way of seeing good in everything she talked of.

The Count was quieter than he had been on the previous night. Dan merely thought he was giving him and Anastasia a change to get to know each other.

Early next morning Dan made his way downstairs to the dining room. The Count was talking to two servants whom Dan did not recognise. Dismissing them the Count then joined Dan for a light breakfast, making a little small talk about the weather and last night's mists.

After breakfast the Count informed Dan that it was time to get to know his way around the castle and the Count's work rooms. They descended to what Dan thought must be the old cellar level, it was something of a labarynth, getting lost in there could take forever to find you're way out.

Opening a large iron door the Count showed Dan into the first workroom. He was staggered, he had expected a dungeon like work room. This was a low ceilinged laboratory tiled in shining white ceramics from floor to ceiling, benches and shelves covered with electronic equipment for mixing and weighing, and a shelf unit on one wall with enough weird and wonderful shaped glassware to set up a shop.

"This, Dan, is my basic research and testing laboratory."

The room that the next door led to was equally as clinical but looked like a vet's operating room to which Dan immediately made reference.

"A perfect observation Dan, that is exactly what it is. You see I do some testing on animals, it is an essential part of my programme, without it my work would be a total waste of time and energy, though I do hope you are not going to get moralistic with me. I can assure you all the tests I do, I do as humanely as possible."

"That sounds reasonable to me." said Dan. "Though I have never done anything like this before, you'll have to teach me from scratch."

"Ah, Dan, I'm sure you'll adapt quickly."

The next set of doors led to another room full of small cages with mice, rats and a selection of rabbits and chickens. At the end of this room were two sets of doors both heavily padlocked.

"So much security down here Count." Dan seemed puzzled as to why the Count had so many precautions."

"You'll see soon enough Dan, suffice to say for now it is better to be safe than sorry. I keep some other specimens which can be a little dangerous at times. It wouldn't do to have them escaping and running around the castle for our own safety. This other is my special library and you shall have to prove yourself before you get a look in there."

By the time two weeks had gone by Dan was becoming accustomed to the work they were doing. Basically simple task in and around the laboratory, weighing and feeding the research animals. By this time the Count had taught him how to take blood samples from most of the animals, but the mixing of chemicals and potions for injection, the Count kept careful control over, always administering to each test animal himself. Late evenings he would enter the padlocked rooms, sometimes being alone until the following morning.

It was these times Dan spent most of the time in Anastasia's company. Their friendship was becoming stronger each day.

On one evening of the third week the Count took Dan aside after dinner.

"Dan, I must speak with you on a matter of some delicacy, I do not wish to interfere with your private thoughts but you must promise me that your friendship with my sister stays just that even if she declares her feelings as stronger towards you must resist. I'll say no more of the matter now but if you must succumb to your urges one or two of the young servants would, I'm sure, be more than happy to oblige you."

"Rest assured Count my word to you is my bond."

"Thank you Dan. Now a brandy to mark the occasion, for tomorrow you shall see the rest of my laboratories and the alchemy library."

Dan was eager to question the Count further on what lay ahead but knew him well enough now to bide his time and let the Count dictate the pace of his learning.

They had spent quite a few mornings out riding so much so that Dan was becoming quite a proficient horseman but not this morning. Dan was impatient to learn the secrets to be revealed to him from behind the padlocked doors of the laboratory.

Dan was tense as they made their way through the clinical brightness of the laboratories until there stood the doors.

Unlocking the left hand room first the Count led Dan through a stone walled passage to another room equally secured with locks, when these were opened they stepped into a high ceilinged room that looked like something that ought to belong to Merlin in King Arthur's time. Dan gasped.

From floor to ceiling were shelves of books, some so old they looked beyond being handled, wooden ladders reached up to shelves fifteen feet high stacked with volume after volume. In the centre of the room was a large leatherbound desk with even more books neatly piled upon it. At the opposite end of the room was another doorway through this they now passed.

Dan could not believe his eyes, if anything this room was even older, the only thing he could think of it resembling was a mediaeval apothecary's; benches and bottles, shelved pots, jars with all distinct markings, none of which Dan could decipher.

"In these rooms, Dan, my family have passed secrets from father to son for a thousand years, you see it the first not of the Versipellis bloodline."

"You do me a great honour Count, it is fantastic, I don't know what else to say. Amazing."

"If you can begin to learn a millionth part of the knowledge in these rooms, Dan, you will become enlightened to a world far beyond that of the cretins and bigots of so-called modern society. This is why you must pledge me your life to our secrecy. Do I have it, Dan?"

"Count, you have it with my soul that I owe you."

"Thank you Dan, that was well phrased, I think we shall achieve much together."

They left the rooms; re-entering the laboratory the Count locked the padlocks and told Dan he would have another set of keys made for him.

Then taking out another bunch of keys the Count started to unlock the other doors. As the door swung open Dan could make out nothing other than a stone walled chamber, cold and a little damp.

Entering, the Count let Dan in behind him, taking a pitch torch from a rack on the wall, he lit it bursting into an orange low that made the shadows flicker and dance on damp stone walls.

"Count, I thought this was a special room, its . . . . its empty."

"Close the door behind you Dan."

As Dan pulled the door to the Count moved to the wall opposite the doorway and seemed to just stare at the stone. Reaching out his left hand he seemed only to touch a single point just above waist level and immediately stepped back as a narrow doorway appeared, stone and wall swinging silently inward. When the door had stopped the Count, torch held at arm's length in front of him, led through descending steep narrow steps until Dan thought they must be fifty feet beneath the basement level of the laboratories.

"You are now in the catacombs, beneath the castle, inside the mountain. These tunnels lead all over the mountains and some go beyond, all exits have hidden locks and latches. Be careful, Dan, in here if you lose yourself you could wander for eternity, lost."

Ten yards from the bottom of the stairs the Count lit another torch in its bracket on the wall and repeated his actions with torches at fifteen foot intervals. This gave an eerie glow to the damp winding walls revealing many wooden doors set in archways.

"These were the dungeons at one time Dan, although we still find usages for some of them here."

Drawing back a huge bolt on one of the wooden doors the Count eased it open. Dan jumped back startled as a dozen huge hounds bounded out into the chamber. Calling to the dogs the Count made them all sit instantly.

"These Dan are but a few of my hunting hounds, I have three times as many in other rooms, all at different levels of awareness. you see part of my work includes heightening of the senses."

Dan had calmed down after his initial reaction. "Is it OK to stroke them?" he asked the Count.

"Walk slowly amongst us Dan but they are not pets to be petted. Let them know your smell for they must learn to trust you if we are to work together."

This action was repeated at five more different rooms, returning all of the hounds to their respective quarters before allowing out the next. Dan couldn't help noticing that each pack was different to each other in ways that seemed obvious, but Dan couldn't say quite why.

"Don't worry Dan, you will soon learn to see the changes in them."

Chapter 3

A VISIT TO THE CITY

❧

DAN HAD SETTLED into a nice routine riding most mornings, sometimes with the Count, sometimes with Anastasia. His afternoons were busy, mostly in the lab where the Count taught him to use the equipment such as his chromatograph, and test serums and blood samples on the electronmicroscope, he also took regular blood samples from the dogs. Although he never really understood just what he was doing he found his work interesting. In the evenings when he was not with the dogs in the catacombs he would be usually found socialising with the Count, though more often than not he sat with Anastasia either chatting or listening to her play the piano.

"We need to take the bull by the horns." The Count announced while he and Dan were out riding in the early morning.

"What do you mean Count?"

"I mean all our experiments, years of work, modern chemistry and technology and what do we have to show for it all, a pack of hybrid dogs no more."

The Count reined in his horse and dismounted even though they were right on the edge of a thick patch of woodland he had warned Dan to stay clear of.

"Count, is it safe to stop here?" Dan's horse was stomping and obviously nervous of something it could sense.

"Ah! there comes a time when we must throw caution to hell, we have to become ruthless in our efforts to find the answers."

"Is there any way I can help you?" Dan asked, as he too dismounted and tried to calm his horse.

"You could, Dan, but it may be dangerous. I have to know what effect the serums evoke in the mind, so it stands to reason that it must be tested on someone who can tell me what is happening inside his head, but there are risks involved."

The Count seemed lost in thought for a time. Dan had grasped what he meant but was puzzled, not fully understanding where the Count's experiments were supposed to lead.

"Maybe if I understood more of what you mean to achieve."

The Count turned at Dan's words. "Yes, yes, you must, we shall find a way. Come let's return home, I shall show you what my true purpose is. I think you may be ready."

Upon their return to the castle they neglected breakfast and the Count led Dan straight down to the alchemy room. Picking up an armful of ancient manuscripts they returned to the dining hall where the Count laid the scripts out on the table. He rummaged through them until he found the one he wanted.

"This Dan, dates back a thousand years of history and research." The Count then began to relate his ancestral tale to Dan.

"Stanislav, the first Count of Versipellis was made Count by Meisko the First for his valour and military aid when this country was first settling. Though he sought solitude to escape the rumours of his involvement with demons suspected of being werewolves. Do you know the very name Versepellis means turnskin from Roman times. Anyone suspected was usually burned alive with all members of their blood in an attempt to kill off the curse. But Stanislav was too powerful and too influential with Meisko for anyone to openly accuse him directly. He set about combing the countryside looking for men and families accused of being werewolves, many of which he found and brought here imprisoning them in these dungeons.

As I have told you he was a practicing alchemist and in these manuscripts are the first notes of his research into the minds and senses of both man and animal.

You must realise in those times simply to survive people had to be cruel and Stanislav was no exception. He kept dozens of specimens most of which died in torment, but his passion for knowledge and his pursuit of his work was unquenchable. This passion is inherent and the male descendants have always continued his work, some coming so close to actually combining the mind of a man to the senses of a beast.

"Look at the tapestries, these are not ordinary hunting scenes, man running with dogs, not following them but leading them. In ancient times these were men who ran with wolves, they survived by virtue of favour from the wolves, men would be the lure for prey and the wolves would tolerate the man until such time that they could no longer keep up with the pack. Many men like this were caught by hunters and villagers, this was Stanislav's prime source of victims for his research."

"He also took in condemned prisoners, an endless supply of research material. You see in those days people believed in far more supernatural things than they do now. People were fearful of all sorts of things merely thought of as fairy tales and folklore legends by the people of to-day. But, I don't think the nearest prison is likely to give us a few condemned men to do a little research on, do you? Neither could we get hold of mental patients from an asylum, besides we need someone who can tell us coherently of their symptoms and feelings."

"You see, many of my ancestors were successful in inducing a state of enhanced awareness of the senses but always this left its toll on the brain of the human. Some simply went mad, some were given to fits and rages of extreme aggression displaying unnatural feats of speed and strength similar to those told of in Icelandic legends. They called them berserkers and used them as fearless bloodthirsty warriors."

"The specimens of greatest interest to the Count were those who showed signs of lycanthropy. They actually believed themselves to transform from man to wolf, these were the ones who learnt to run with the dogs. Some specimens showing abilities far above those of an ordinary hunting dog, but none of these survived for very long. It seemed as if the higher the senses the shorter the lifespan, or maybe there was simply too great a build-up of toxins in the body for it to survive."

"These are the answers I need to find, with modern analysis equipment I can test for toxins and create man in hybrid form, but you see how difficult it is with just animals to work on."

"A thousand year's research in pursuit of creating the ultimate man only to be beaten by simple minded bigots with such high moral values that they would rather wipe themselves out in striving to become civilised, this is not nature's balance but simply the greed of mankind. Animals are not greedy, where and when did it creep into man's nature? You see to go forward man must go backward. We have to find a way to acquire some specimens to work with, but without drawing attention I'm not sure how."

Both the Count and Dan sat in silence for some time. The Count rose and poured them both large glasses of brandy. Dan also rose and offered a toast with the Count.

"To find a way to success."

The Count replied "We must Dan, we must."

Dan walked around the room studying tapestries with a much greater understanding. One in particular caught his attention more than the others, "Count" Dan called from the far end of the room. "This tapestry, what" before he had finished the question the count answered.

"That is Stanislav the First procuring his specimens. It was said that a family of vicious robbers and villains were terrorising some villages, Stanislav simply branded them as werewolves and had them rounded up. Most died before capture but that didn't worry the villagers. Either way they had been done a great service, both they and Stanislav had what they wanted."

Dan seemed deep in thought then spoke quietly to the Count.

"Could we not do the same, on a much smaller and quieter scale, of course?"

The Count gave Dan a long thoughtful look almost staring right through him.

"You may have something there Dan, you just may."

At that moment Anastasia walked in "Here you are, I've been looking for you two. I've decided I would like to take a trip to the city, would either of you two mad scientists like to accompany me?"

"My dear sister, what a wonderful idea."

"Count, I don't think it is wise for me to be abroad in the city, I am a wanted man remember." Dan said quietly enough for only the Count to hear.

The Count asked Dan to take a look at himself "You now have a beard, your hair is a little longer, your dress is that of a Pole, your mother would not recognise you and besides you would be with me. I am a nobleman here you know and nobody would dare question the company I wish to keep. Besides, we can test you're theory for procuring some new research material, yes?"

"Well yes Count if you think it's safe I'll come along." answered Dan a little hesitantly.

That evening all Anastasia could talk about was the following day's trip and just what she should take with her. "We have to stay a few days at least." she announced at dinner. "I simply can't do enough in one day."

"Very well sister, that suits our plans. We may even stay a little longer if we feel the need."

The Count called for Mishcow and gave him instructions to inform the Vigor Hotel in Warsaw that he wished a suite of rooms preparing for himself and guests including a member of staff, on a private floor, for an indefinite period, though probably no more than one week.

The next morning Miscow brought the shining black Mercedes limousine out into the courtyard while the Count made Anastasia take back at least half the luggage she intended to bring. The Count had provided Dan with several suits of clothes most of which packed neatly into one suitcase, his own requirements being must the same, although the suits were a little more ostentatious in style, but then he was a real Count, Dan thought.

They arrived in the hotel in late evening and were graciously ushered to their suite. It was on the top floor and was very elegant by comparison to anywhere Dan had ever been and not a single form to fill in, or question asked. This kind of attention appealed to Dan as he did feel a little nervous outside the comparative safety of the castle. They settled in to their rooms, washed and changed ready to go out for a late dinner.

Anastasia came into the living room quarters from her bedroom looking radiant, if a little flustered. Dan and the Count had been waiting half an hour.

"Oh! don't rush me Manfred." The Count gave her his cold glare. "Dear brother, can we go to Hussars. I do so like it there and we ought to show Dan some of the sights of our country's capital city."

"Very well, Anna, I must admit Hussars does have a good reputation. The food is excellent, but Dan does not have to see all Warsaw in one night, so do control your excitement." The Count's tone was pleasant but firm.

The evening was taken up by a horse pulled carriage ride all over the city stopping in the Old Town market square for dinner at Hussars Restaurant and drinks at several charming taverns. Returning to the hotel they sat up late getting through several 'Just one more' nightcaps.

While Anastasia was mostly flitting here and there, Dan and the Count wandered the quieter and seedier areas of the city inconspicuously watching the comings and going of many. Several crowds of rowdy tourists caught their interest though tourists were sometimes easily missed and rarely travelled alone. They strayed into bars more frequented by what you could only describe as the more criminal element of Warsaw's society. Rogues and villains who would ask no questions and give no quarter, surely they thought no one would miss one of these scoundrels. It simply remained to select one then find a method of getting him back to the castle undetected.

That evening after dinner the trio returned much earlier to the hotel. The Count told Anastasia that he and Dan had a little business to take care of. They changed into plainer more drab clothes than their usual elegant apparel and bidding Anastasia goodnight, left the hotel undetected, exiting by the rear staircase.

Making their way to a tavern on the other side of the city by way of a good crisp walking pace they did not want to take taxis or any other form of transport where they might be remembered.

It took them forty-five minutes to reach the part of the city they wanted. Entering the crowded tavern they sat in a corner and ordered drinks. After fifteen minutes or so they were approached by a young hard-looking man in an old shabby coat. He sat opposite Dan, his cold eyes seemed to bore right through Dan.

The Count talked to him in hushed tones, Dan couldn't catch a single word of it, he just sat and pretended he understood as the Count had told him, though he was aware of the gist of the conversation as he and the Count had planned it out together that afternoon.

The Count passed a twenty thousand zloty note to the man, taking hold of his hand as he clutched the note and in a cold hard tone told the man.

"Do not cross me, tell on one, I'll see you tomorrow night behind this tavern there could be a lot more money for you if you do the job well."

With that last comment the Count and Dan rose and left the tavern again walking back to the hotel's rear entrance, making sure they were not followed.

The man, a thief by nature, shunned by most who knew him in Warsaw also left the tavern. As the Count had instructed him not to spend any of the money given to him in the same tavern where they may have been seen together, though he did go straight to another equally disreputable establishment and proceed to get drunk. Some people who knew him asked where his money had come from but he remembered the Count's warning and the promise of more money for what he thought would be a little thievery and kept his mouth shut.

All the next day Anastasia complained at having to go home at such short notice. She had wanted to show Dan more of the "Wonderful Capital" as she put it, but the Count was adamant.

Settling the hotel bill they checked out at seven o'clock that evening. Mishcow waited in the car while they went out to a tavern and then on to Hussars for a meal.

Mishcow had been informed by the Count of what was expected of him later that night and was ready with the car and two raincoats having cleared ample space in the boot of the limousine for what was needed.

He picked them up from Hussars at ten-twenty and drove to a quiet back street and parked. Anastasia had fallen asleep in the plush leather seat of the limousine helped to relax a little by the sleeping potion the Count had dropped into her last drink in Hussars.

Dan and the Count went around to the back of the limousine, opening the boot and taking out the two raincoats they put them on over their suits. Dan picked a small bottle and a patch of heavy lint cloth from a small box while the Count removed a syringe and checked its contents by the courtesy light in the boot of the Mercedes. Closing the boot they both concealed the items they were carrying and made their way down a dark street to the alleyway where they had planned to meet the thief.

As they turned into the alley he was there a few yards down behind the tavern.

Dan looked over his shoulder to see if there was anyone about. Some people were passing at the tope of the street where the limousine was parked but not a soul any closer than that.

Dan's heart raced as he approached the thief. While the Count engaged him in quiet conversation Dan loosened the lid of the bottle with his thumb and fore finger whilst it was still in his pocket. With the other hand he grasped the lint. When he felt the top fall from the bottle inside his pocket he gave an almost unnoticeable cough, more than simply the clearing of his throat.

The Count noticed Dan's signal that he was ready. Slowly he moved sideways holding the thief's attention, turning his back on Dan, taking out a wad of notes from his pocket to distract him. As soon as Dan saw the money he was now behind the thief, he withdrew the bottle from his pocket and quickly soaked the lint clasping a cloth over the thief's note and mouth. Instantly, the Count grabbed the struggling man and held him fast clamping his arms to his sides. In no more than a few seconds he had started to go limp. Letting him slip to the ground Dan replaced the cap on the bottle of Chloroform and stuffed both bottle and cloth into his raincoat pocket.

The Count ran up to the top of the alley and waved, then returned to Dan and their victim. The Count then pushed up the sleeve on one of the thief's arms and deftly inserted the syringe into an accommodating vein sending the powerful narcotic into his system. It would be at least twentyfour hours before this one stares, he thought to himself.

Mishcow pulled the limousine to a halt in the alley opening the boot from a button inside on the dashboard while Dan and the Count carried the limp body of the thief and dumped him down in the space left in the limousine's boot. Stripping off their raincoats they were also deposited in the boot before it was closed and locked.

The Count and Dan, both sweating, climbed into the rear of the car, joining the sleeping Anastasia as Mishcow drove sedately away set for a long night's drive home to the castle.

Chapter 4

INVESTIGATION

꘡

KEITH STUBB'S 'PHONE rang at 3.20am. "Stubbs? the voice on the other end of the 'phone paused until Stubbs answered coherently. "Got one right up your street here, get yourself down to the Municipal Park just behind Lacey Street. We've got a body with its throat ripped right out."

Stubbs hung up the 'phone, dressed and made his way wearily to the crime scene.

Keith Stubbs was a big man, standing about six feel tall, weighing around sixteen stone, carrying little excess fat even though he took virtually no exercise, with dark shaggy unkempt hair and a full greying beard.

"Got any witness, Sergeant?" Stubbs asked.

"Two youths, they are at the station now, Inspector."

Stubbs walked over to where the body lay and poked around in the nearby bushes. Turning up nothing he then asked the doctor who was examining the body if he had any ideas how he was killed and what the time of death was. The doctor commented quite sarcastically.

"Yes, around midnight, he's had his throat ripped out."

"Yeh, yeh." Stubbs either missed the sarcasm or simply ignored it.

"Ripped out, but how and what with?"

"By the looks of it, Inspector, by a bare hand and brute force, I'll have more for you tomorrow."

As the body was taken away Stubbs dismissed the rest of the policemen who were standing about and informed them he was going back to the station to question the youths. The two youths had checked out to have previous records and convictions for assault and robbery so Stubbs was not inclined to believe their story that one man had come out of the bushes and attacked three for no apparent reason, although that was not what he felt mattered at that moment. What did matter was he had a description of a man wanted for a killing that the press were going to love.

At five o'clock he went home intending to try to get at least two hour's sleep before his day started.

The papers did have a field day, especially those which tend to sensationalise. Reports of a monster in the park and a beast attack were followed up by articles criticising the police for turning up nothing more than one possible suspect, a stolen car, and some stolen money which may or may not be connected; although the suspect, a Mr Daniel Hunter, had disappeared somewhere on the continent, his last known whereabouts being the Zebrugge ferry terminal.

The flack he was getting didn't both Stubbs any, he was used to people either having a go at him or yakking behind his back. Even when he came to work the English police force fifteen year's ago he came under a cloud though it was a subject he never spoke of himself.

Nobody had ever got the full story. It seemed when he was a young rookie mountie in the Canadian Mounted Police Force (Stubbs originally being a French Canadian) he had accompanied a senior officer in bringing in a felon from a remote outpost somewhere in the mountains in Quebec. Having taken custody of the prisoner the three men set out for home, a long trek across country only manageable by man and horse, no vehicle being able to make the trip into the mountains.

Over two months later Stubbs appears in a small town at the base of the mountains barely alive, covered in bites, scars and open wounds, none of which were recognised as anything known to be like that of any of the local wildlife which happened to include almost everything that lives and eats flesh on that Continent.

All they ever got out of Stubbs was that he lived off the land after they were attacked by wild animals in the dead of the night whilst making camp in a woodland clearing.

Some of the few people who have ever called on Stubb's home had commented that was probably why he had a morbid fascination for woodland and folklore stories of which books had a house full. It was also probably why he got the gruesome jobs as nothing ever seemed to turn his stomach, or upset him personally.

Two months later the case having been simply left unsolved Stubbs was called into the office.

"You wanted to see me Keith?" Stubbs came through the door without knocking as usual.

"Ah! Stubbs, yes, we've got a break in the park-Hunter case. It seems the car has turned up in Poland stolen by some village urchin or something."

"Well, that's a big lead, Chief, what do I do go to Poland and fingerprint it after it's been gone two months."

"Hang on, Keith, that's not all—there's a dead male carrying Hunter's I.D. and it appears the Police in a place called Krakow have a passport belonging to our Mr Daniel Hunter, but the dead male is not our boy, it seems he was knifed in a brawl. So I've arranged for you to go on a nice little flight to Krakow. You can get there direct from Heathrow tomorrow and there will be a representative of the Polish

Police Force who is also a qualified translator there to meet you. You are to work together in the best interests in our new East/West harmonious relations and, if you can, bring that bugger home and let's get this poxy file off our backs. Draw some funds from accounts and change it at the bank this afternoon. I've already called to see and they will have your Zlotys ready for you. Harris can look after your work while you're gone."

"Do I have a choice, Chief?"

"Frankly, Keith, no. Take this afternoon off and get yourself sorted out. Your plan tickets will be ready at the check-in at the airport. Your flight times 9.30am. And one other think, don't . . . ."

Stubbs cut in abruptly with a cold glare in his eyes. "Don't say it Chief, that was a long time ago."

The Chief looked as if he wished he could have hidden from the look Stubbs had given him. "OK, Keith, but be careful and take it easy."

With that Stubbs turned and left the office. On his way out he stopped at his desk sorting out one or two notes then spoke to Harris for about twenty minutes about his pending cases.

"Nothing you can't handle mate." Stubbs said to Harris with a wry smile on his face. "See you when I get back."

When Stubbs arrived at Krakow airport he was met by a uniformed policeman no more than twenty-two. A bright, cheerful young man by the name of Nicoleyevich Ochep. Not quite as tall as Stubbs and so thin as to look undernourished, his English was excellent despite the heavy accent. He informed Stubbs that he had mastered in four other languages as well and he hoped one day to be chosen for international service in an ever increasingly united Europe.

"Good for you." Stubbs commented though whether merely as a gesture of good manners or whether genuine he could not tell from his tone. "Would you mind if I call you Niko as Nicoleyevich is a bit of a mouthful?"

"By all means Inspector" said Nico "Vud you like to freshen up before we report to the station?"

"No let's get on with it, I'll settle down later." Stubbs had only one small kit bag with him, he always felt more comfortable unburdened and hated carrying anything for too long. Besides a change of clothes in his bag he had his old 38 Police special revolver, something he had held on to since his rookie days in the Mounties, although his peers in the British force knew nothing of its existence.

On arriving at Police Headquarters the formal introductions being over with, the first thing Stubbs wanted to do was examine the body which he immediately realised was definitely not Daniel Hunter. This man was at least six foot two, blonde, and didn't even look English.

"Looks more like a crou . . . ahem German to me." Stubbs just correcting himself in time not to offend. They then returned to the police station where Stubbs was shown Dan's arrest reports. Niko translated the script for him, he then explained to Stubbs that his superiors felt they now realised why he did not wish to return to collect his passport and see the judge, he must have thought they would be straight on to him. Listening to everything being repeated in both languages was beginning to grate on Stubb's nerves.

"Can I see the man you arrested with the car now? I think that's going to be our best lead." Niko spoke to his superiors for a few minutes more then turned back to Stubbs.

"Vell, Sir."

"Don't call me Sir, Keith will do nicely, thanks."

"Yes, er Keith, Sir, it seems he is not here, I'm afraid ve do have him but he is in a small town station near Oswiecim.

Niko took Stubbs to a small hotel in the suburbs of Krakow telling him everything was arranged for him to visit the prisoner, Jozef Jaruzaski, tomorrow morning. Niko would pick him up from his hotel at eight o'clock and drive him to Oswiecim.

After Stubbs was checked into a hotel Niko asked if he would like to accompany him for the evening.

"No, you take the night off, I'll manage to get a drink and a meal one way or another. if anything Stubbs was resourceful even if he couldn't speak the local language, besides he preferred his own company most of the time anyway.

As good as his word Stubbs managed to procure a decent meal and a few drinks for himself before retiring to his room for the night and was ready when Niko came for him at seven fifteen am.

The journey to Oswiecim police station was uneventful, although the unmarked police car they travelled in could have been a little more comfortable Stubbs thought on more than one occasion.

On arriving at the police station they sat in a small freshly painted interview room. Jozef Jaruzelski sat opposite Niko and Stubbs.

He was a young man and Stubbs felt a pang of sorrow immediately upon meeting him. Jozef was obviously very poor and very frightened, bewildered as to why stealing a car could be such an important crime, but then he was unaware of whose property he had taken although he had thought at the time such a car probably belonged to a servant and would be of no consequence to a nobleman of Count Versipellis' standing. He had been in the village near the Count's castle when he had heard that the Count was in Warsaw for a week. He had sneaked up to the castle to see what he could pilfer and had found the car in an old unlocked barn by the stables and thought to sell if off cheaply in the city.

THE STORY OF THIS BOOK

TURNSKIN
BY STEVEN HAMMONDS.

CONCIEVED IN 1993, THE MANUSCRIPT
WAS UNBALANCED AND FOR TEN
YEARS LAY UNFINISHED.
IN 2003 I SUFFERED A STROKE
FROM THE RESULT OF AN OPPERATION
THE SURGEON SUGGESTED THAT I WOULD
PROBEBALLY NOT REGAIN FULLY MY
ABILITY OF SPEECH AND USE OF READING
AND WRITING.
THIS LEFT ME DETERMIND TO BEAT
THIS AFFLICTION.
IT HAS TAKEN TEN MORE YEARS TO HAVE
THIS BOOK READY TO PUBLISH, EVEN
THOUGH MY SPELLING AND GRAMMER
ARE POOR. I LEAVE THESE MISTAKES IN
TO INSPIRE PEOPLE WHO HAVE
SUFFERED SIMILARLEY,
AND AS I
TO NEVER GIVE UP
YOURS STEVEN. HAMMONDS

The keys being in the ignition had made the temptation to take the car too great. Why it had caused such a fuss to get him locked up for more than a week and to have an English investigator come all the way to Oswiecim had him puzzled. His dilemma was whether he could lie his way out, or simply admit sealing from the reclusive Count.

Jozef was terrified as Stubb sat opposite him, his eyes seeming to burn into his very thoughts.

"These are a simple people, Keith, easily intimidated, especially by someone as experienced as yourself. I will do my best to interpret his words accurately."

Stubbs thanked Niko and returned to the conversation saying "We will make him sweat a little first."

"Yes sir."

Niko was just as transfixed by Stubbs' manner as was Jozef Jaruzelski. It didn't take Stubbs a great deal of time to extract Jozef's story from him though it would have been easier without the efforts of translating everything.

The gist of the story was that Jozef whilst in Zywiec had heard that the Count was visiting Warsaw so he sneaked up to the castle to snoop around. Being unable to gain access to the interior of the castle without a forcible entry, he plumped for the easier task of searching through the outbuildings and barns.

When he had found the Lada with its keys he had intended to drive it to a friend who would most likely give him a good price for it in Katowice but it had overheated and he had been stopped by the police on the outskirts of Oswiecim. What scared him was not the fear of the police but of retribution of Count Versipellis.

At the end of his confessions he begged to be punished for his thievery but pleaded that the Count should not discover his identity.

Stubbs had seen a lot of frightened and tormented people in his career but never one so abjectly fearful of one person, even during investigations involving gang land informers and syndicate dealings in his experiences with the English and Canadian police.

As they left the police station in Oswiecim Stubbs said to Nico. "I would like to visit this Count chap, can we go there now?"

Nico seemed a little stuck for words. "I think we had better go through the proper channels, sir. After all Count Versipellis is a nobleman of great Polish ancestry."

Stubbs' reaction to that was to say the least blunt. One translation Nico was not too sure of.

Back at the police headquarters Stubbs was getting annoyed with red tape, browbeating Nico into embarrassing translations with statements such as, "If this Count has had Hunter's car stored at his place the last thing I want to do is warn him of my intention to question him. Just because he is a damn Count doesn't put him above reproach you know."

After waiting around for several hours Stubbs finally got the go ahead to visit the Count unannounced although they would not guarantee him an audience and today was out of the question as, by the time they could have reached the Count's castle, it would be night time and there were no local hotels or establishments to accommodate an overnight stay as such a journey would require.

"You see, it is right in the mountains, the Count is very much a recluse, Inspector Stubbs." Niko was being very formal as his superiors were present.

"Then we leave for the Count's first thing tomorrow. Can you pick me up early, Niko?" Niko's reply was as always polite and accommodating.

Stubbs and Niko arrived at the castle by midday. Parking the unmarked police car in the courtyard Niko, dressed in his uniform, stepped up to the grand carved wooden doorway and pulled hesitantly on the bell chain.

Mishcow answered the door, where upon Niko showed his identification to Mishcow. The two then spoke together for a few minutes, none of which Stubbs could understand. Eventually they were shown into the castle and asked to wait in the large reception room where Dan had waited some months earlier. Leaving the two policemen together Mishcow left the room closing the door behind him.

"What was all that about Niko?"

"The butler said that the Count does not usually see anyone without an appointment. I had to push him into trying to get us an audience with the Count by stressing the seriousness of your enquiries. He said he would ask."

"Jeez! Niko does this Count think he is above the law or something?"

"In some ways Inspector, he probably does."

Niko was waiting for Stubbs to continue his complaining over the diplomatic situation but the comments he expected never cam.

Stubbs had wandered off and was engrossed in studying the various tapestries and paintings that hung in the great room.

"My God." Stubbs kept repeating to himself as he wandered around the room studying the tapestries. "Niko."

"What is it Inspector?"

"What did you say this Count's name was?"

"It is Count Manfred Versipellis, Inspector."

Stubbs stood shaking his head like he did not believe what he was seeing. Niko was totally puzzled by Stubbs' reaction to the room but thought better of it than to ask what it was that had taken his interest so greatly.

Stubbs then asked Niko "How much do you know about this guy and what he does?"

Stubbs paused looking again at the tapestries. The name Versipellis had now stirred a thought within him, he recognised it from somewhere, but could not quite remember where. He was convinced it was something to do with his knowledge of folklore as these tapestries certainly were, those he fully understood.

Stubbs was still engrossed when Mishcow opened the door.

Standing in the doorway was the Count exactly as Stubbs had imagines him. Taller than Stubbs with a regal bearing and long greying hair. Niko bowed and introduced himself and Stubbs very formally in Polish.

Stubbs was surprised by the clarity of the Count's English as he spoke. "Welcome gentlemen, I think in honour of our distinguished English detective we ought to speak in his own language. Now how may I help you?"

Stubbs initially stumbled over how to address the Count.

"Well sir, er' Count I am investigating a possible murder case committed some months ago in England. It appears a vehicle we believe possible connected to the case was stolen by a local small time thief from these very premises. Can you tell me anything about this?"

"Well, Inspector". the Count was so calm and reserved, one of the few men that Stubbs had difficulty in judging accurately on first impressions. "My servants inform me that we hired a handyman about a month ago. It seems he arrived in this car. He proved unsuitable for the duties we required him for so he was dismissed. When he left he told my butler Mishcow that the car was faulty and asked if he may return in a day or so with a friend to tow it away. Mishcow had agreed to his request and told him to leave it in the disused barn near the stables. I was under the impression that he had simply returned and taken it away with him."

Stubbs found the Count's story very convincing but something inside told him not to believe it.

"Do you mind if I take a look at the barn in question?"

"By all means, Inspector, and if that is all I will bid you farewell. Mishcow will show you the barn before you leave. Now if you will excuse me I am a busy man, good day gentlemen."

The finality of the Count's tone sent Stubbs into one of his obstinate moods.

"But, I may have one or two more questions to ask after seeing the barn."

The Count did not show any reaction to Stubbs' obvious change of tone but simply answered. "If you have anything more to ask Mishcow will answer them for you, besides he knows more of the comings and goings of servants, good day to you."

Without waiting for an answer the Count turned and strode out of the room. Mishcow then appeared and once more Stubbs had to rely on Niko to translate for him.

Although there was not much to see in the barn, Mishcow gave Niko the name and address of the handyman leaving both Stubbs and Niko nothing more to do than start on the long drive back to the police headquarters and check out the name Mishcow had given them.

Back in Kracow the local police turned up nothing on the man in question. Stubbs waited around for a week while the local police proceeded with further enquiries into the identity of the so called handyman. At the end of the week Stubbs wondered if the man had ever existed at all. The Polish Police Chief told Stubbs that there was nothing more they could do for him.

"So that's it them, we don't seem to have got very far, do we?" Stubbs complained.

His attempts to get them to let him question the Count again were answered with a definite but diplomatic no. Stubbs guessed that the Police Chief's grammar had lost something in its translation.

The next day found Stubbs writing out his report on the flight home. Since Stubbs had entered the Count's reception room something had started to eat away at him, stirring his curiosity into overdrive.

Niko with a little prompting had told Stubbs what he knew of the Count which was not much other than that he was a descendant of a line of highlyranked noble men and was educated in England. Stubbs didn't think for one minute that the Chief back in England would let him follow-up his hunches by investigating a foreign diplomat, but he could always make some enquiries discreetly in his own time.

Over the next few weeks Stubbs did some poking around, unofficially, of course. The information he succeeded in accumulating on the Count was not a great deal but he felt it was worth its weight in gold.

Twenty years ago a visiting Polish nobleman studying medicine at the London College of Medicine had left under a cloud just before taking his final exams. The College had accused him of illegal use and sale of narcotic drugs to fellow students. This was not easily obtained information as the whole scandal was kept quiet for political reasons. Although, eventually Stubbs had managed to track down one of the Count's participating students now working as a G.P. in the Midlands, Stubbs had managed to arrange a week-end off and decided to pay a visit, unofficially, of course.

Dr Jarvis Lang greeted Stubbs cordially though he claimed he could not remember a great deal of twenty years ago as a student. Although two things he mentioned gave Stubbs a line on what he had suspected all along. It appears that the Count had tricked several fellow students into trying a particular drug which he had produced in the laboratory he had installed in the basement of the house he rented in London.

The Count had claimed it would raise ones sense of awareness, but all hell broke loose when one student developed what was thought to be a case of schizophrenia though later on diagnosed as possibly lycantropy. Dr Lang emphasised only possibly a mild form of lycanthropy. The student in question had shortly afterwards taken his own life.

Dr Lang also told Stubbs that just before his demise he had spoken to him whereupon he had claimed to actually change into an animal at any given time of night or day.

At the time of the incident other students simply accused the Count of nothing more than serving up a little L. S. D. When the young man had died the Count had diplomatically asked to leave and the scandal was soon forgotten.

The College authorities wanted no news of events to leak out. Those who were involved were told to keep quiet about events or face expulsion and possible prosecution. Everyone kept quiet.

Stubbs then reassured Dr Lang that this whole conversation was off the record and would certainly not be repeated byhim. It was merely a little background information for his own enquiries. Dr Lang would never be mentioned in anyway, Stubbs gave his word.

On his way home rather than be satisfied with what he had learned, Stubbs now felt his curiosity grow to an insatiable desire to find out more about this Count Versipellis.

Back at home he checked through some of his books dwelling on passages concerning lycanthropy and its folklore origins. He found part of what he wanted in the Encyclopedia Britannica. Versipellis was from the Roman meaning turnskin, attributed tothose accused of being made into werewolves by means of magic spells or herbs. That was enough for Stubbs, it stirred old memories of a bitter struggle for life and survival. Nothing would quench the burning desire that was now starting to take him over, the desire to find out the truth. He suspected the Count was a werewolf and he intended to find out.

It took him two months to clear his workload and put his personal things in order whilst he arranged for a year's leave of absence saying some family business had made it necessary for him to return to Canada for a time. Then he was ready.

Chapter 5

RESEARCH CONTINUES

❦

D AN WAS WORRIED when the Count told him of the visitors and what had happened over the car. Despite the Count's assurances that he had enough influence over certain diplomatic officials to pressurise high level police officers into packing this nosey English policeman on to the next flight home. Dan was given a little consolation over his worries by Anastasia although she only seemed to show any concern whilst not in her brother's company.

Dan was a little hesitant when confiding anything to Anastasia as he did not know how much the Count had told her, or wanted her to know. the Count's new found enthusiasm for his experiments could not be marred by trifling worries such as Dan's, as he would comment with monotonous regularity.

Down in the dungeons, kept in a chamber near to where the dogs were kept was Jadwiga, the thief. At first they had to keep him quite highly drugged but as time went by he was eased off the sedatives and appeared to accept his fate more easily. He was fed well and often and was starting to show signs of an increase in his sensory awareness, especially while exercising in the tunnels of the catacombs at which time he was always accompanied by Dan, the Count and at least five or six of the dogs, just to ensure that he did not try to escape.

The Count also carried a shock stick, as he called it. When used again Jadwiga it would give him enough of an electric shock to render him helpless for a minute or two without inflicting any serious harm. He soon learnt to do just as he was told.

After a few weeks of the treatments the Count and Dan were having to rely more on the dogs to keep up with Jadwiga as his abilities improved and when questioned by the Count he admitted a distinct increase in his vision, hearing and sense of smell.

The Count also took regular blood tests and tissue samples as a result of which Jadwiga was beginning to look horribly scarred. Dan was reaching a stage now where he was finding this work to be distasteful although he did not dare mention his feelings to the Count.

It was several weeks after this that Jadwiga began to change.

Dan helped the Count in watching Jadwiga more carefully and both decided that it would be too dangerous to let him out to run in the catacombs with only the dogs able to keep up. According to the Count's tests, Jadwiga was suffering from a reaction to the treatments causing a severely distressed mental state, although the fact that he was now chained up probably made a considerable contribution to that condition.

More disturbing though were the physical disorders. He shied away from bright light, but most disconcerting of all was the change in his pigmentation and some of the Count's tests showed massive surges in his hormone levels. His skin was becoming darker and leathery, his eyes and even his teeth and finger nails were turning pinkish. He was beginning to salivate excessively and was prone to lapse into fits and seizures, often followed by a state of complete coma.

The Count was becoming much less social, especially at evening meals and did not bother with their regular early morning rides. He tended to brood and spent hours alone locked in the alchemy room going over the books and manuscripts.

The Count would fly into regular outbursts cursing Jadwiga for being ill-educated and oafish without the mental capacity to understand the basic ideas of his miraculous transformation, claiming that as his senses developed his intelligence shrank.

Dan had little to say to the Count during these outbursts and tended to shy away and leave him to his ravings and tempers on his own, sometimes seeking nothing more than a bottle of wine and the solitude of his room.

It was such an evening after a day of particularly offensive comments from the Count, Dan was sitting alone on his bed having drunk the best part of a decanter of brandy. He rose to shut out the chill draught that blew in from the veranda doors and as Dan turned back towards his bed standing in the centre of the room by the bed was Anastasia, wearing a beautiful white close fitting lace gown which left very little of her ample bosom and figure to the imagination. Dan was surprised but his surprise soon gave way to a feeling of arousal flowing through him.

Anastasia and Dan spent a night of frenzied passion though when Dan woke Anastasia had left the room leaving him a note on his pillow asking him not to say anything of their feelings, or what had happened, to her brother as he was protective and jealous of her. When Dan rose he put the note away in a small drawer inside one of the wardrobes.

That morning at breakfast the Count calmly announced. "We need another specimen, one with a little more intelligence, one that can tell us more of what is happening. This one is deteriorating rapidly.

He is so weak now, at least we no longer need to keep him chained. I think we should do an autopsy immediately."

"But Count, he's not dead is he?" Dan's voice was quavering, the Count sensed he was on edge.

"Not yet, Dan. But surely you must have expected this when we brought him here."

"Of course, Count, I'm just a little off this morning. I'm probably still just a little worried over that Police business."

The Count reassured Dan of his safety in the castle as they made their way down to the laboratories but when they got to the dungeons Jadwiga had gone. All day Dan and the Count searched the Catacombs with the dogs, eventually finding one of the secret mountain exits open.

"It will be dark soon." The Count seemed a little nervous as he spoke, a side to his personality Dan had never seen. "We shall take the dogs and horses out at first light but now lock this gateway, lets re-check these passages."

At day break Dan took two horses from the stables, a bay gelding which he had got used to riding and the Count's grey stallion, to a place in the mountains they had ridden past many times. When he arrived there the Count was waiting with a dozen hounds having made his way through the catacombs leaving by one of the hidden gateways.

Dan and the Count both carried hunting rifles. The Count also wore at his belt a brace of hunting knives and a tranquiliser dart pistol.

The hounds set off at a loping trot searching for the scent of Jadwega. The Count quickly mounted and they set off to hunt down their quarry.

A man with the sense of an animal, it would not be an easy chase, Dan thought. But surely these dogs ought to be able to pick up

Jadweg's scent easily enough. That proved not to be the case, several times the pack picked up a trace only to lose it or confuse it. On several occasions they found small animals mostly devoured but some simply ripped to shreads for no reason.

By mid-day they came to a particularly dense part of a forested slope, too thick to penetrate on horse back. They tied up their horses and cautiously entered the woods, keeping half of the hounds close while the others roamed around searching for a scent.

Their path criss-crossed itself many times and after a couple of hours on foot Dan was exhausted.

"Very well, Dan, you take the dogs and go straight back to the horses, the dogs will lead you back. I will take the others and circle around. Wait with the horses for me, I shouldn't be more than an hour or two."

Dan was nervous, following the two large dogs he jumped and twitched at every sound in the woods. he was almost out of the dense cover of the trees when the dogs suddenly stopped in their tracks. He could see flickers of daylight from the clear land just beyond the trees, what really scared him was that there wasn't a single sound coming from anywhere. Dan was aware of his heart beating at about twice its normal rate. He stood frozen to the spot, his knuckles were white grasping the stock of the hunting rifle he carried. The hounds sniffed the air turning their heads to and fro, ears pricked up then suddenly they took off towards the light.

The tiredness in Dan's legs vanished and he started off after them as fast as he could go, stumbling and tripping over scrub and roots his momentum managing to keep him from falling flat on his face. He burst free from the trees twenty yards from where the horses were then collapsed on the rocky grass breathing raggedly.

Something landed on his back pinning him to the ground instantly. A cold scream tore from his throat, he felt the back of his neck being raked by something sharp. Within seconds the hounds turned and headed straight to him growling and barked. the think on Dan's back stopped tearing at his neck and he felt its weight shift in the middle of his back and it was gone.

The two dogs barking madly ran straight past him as he tried to stretch for the rifle which had fallen on the ground three feet beyond his reach his head was spinning and he could not comprehend what had happened.

Struggling against his desire to drift into unconsciousness he dragged himself almost drunkenly toward where the rifle lay. As his fingers clamped around the gun he heard a rustle from the woods behind him; too weak to turn quickly enough he squeezed off a shot before he passed out.

The Count came out of the woods at a run with the pack surrounding him, to find the two hounds he had left with Dan sitting at Dan's body, their fur matted with blood with large tufts missing. One hound had lost an eye.

The Count instantly checked if Dan was breathing, tearing off his shirt and strapping Dan's wounds he revived Dan with a flask of water from his caddie, then helped him up into the bay's saddle.

By the time they got back to the castle it was almost dark. The servants carried Dan to the surgical room in the laboratory where the Count gave him an injection. Dan was out almost instantly. Anastasia appeared and helped her brother to disinfect and sew up Dan's wounds.

When Dan was settled in his room the Count led the dogs through a small concealed door in the outer wall which led into one of the cells in the catacombs. He settled them down and treated the injured animals before returning to check on Dan's condition.

Anastasia was sat nursing him as the Count entered. "He's still unconscious. Manfred, what happened out there?"

"I don't know Anna, something attacked him while we were separated but I think the dogs drove it off, come let him rest now he's more shaken than badly hurt. He'll be fine in a day or two."

Anastasia wondered if her brother had noticed her reluctance to leave him though he made no comment of it to her. On the third day of his confinement to bed Dan was becoming frustrated by his inactivity, constantly complaining to Anastasia who fussed over him.

As he tried to get up with the help of Anna his head felt like it was full of thick soup, he was shaky and had to sit back down instantly to regain his equilibrium. By the end of the day after half a dozen similar attempts he began to be a little more competent making it to the bathroom where he could carefully wash and refresh himself, even though Ann insisted on not leaving his side at all times.

That evening after the Count had checked his wounds Dan managed to dress and made his way carefully downstairs to dinner catching the Count and Anna unawares, seemingly in the middle of an argument though they both vehemently denied Dan had interrupted them as he excused himself for bursting in on them.

Over dinner Dan had found himself wanting to tell the Count of the disjointed dreams he had as a child which had returned with his accident and confinement to bed but found himself holding back feeling almost fearful of letting his secrets out to this man. He trusted him, but then he had to. Dan's problem, he thought to himself, was simply this trauma of his attack and the residual effect of the medicines the Count had administered to him during his recovery.

Neither the Count nor Anastasia seemed to sense this unease though they cautioned him to take things very easy as he could be a little groggy for a few more days yet.

Dan asked the Count whether he had found any sign of the quarry before his accident. The Count's reply puzzled Dan for a few seconds then he realised that his answer was worded such for Anastasia's sake.

"No, Dan, the animal eluded us that day though I think it was injured, I would not think it to survive long, especially as the weather turns colder as it will soon."

The conversation to'd and fro'd over many subjects, mainly Dan thought the Count's efforts to stop Anna asking too many questions concerning their hunting incident, until finally the Count left the dining table picking up his goblet of wine and announced to Dan that he must soon be fit again as they must procure some more research material. Dan was silent for a few seconds then managed to stutter his reply.

"Er! yes, Count. I will, I will soon be fit."

Dan's stomach churned after all that had happened to Jadwega and his encounter in the woods his desire to help the Count with his work was diminishing rapidly, but worst of all he couldn't help thinking that it may have been Jadwega who had attacked him. The Count assured him whilst in his sickbed that it must have been a bear strayed down from the mountains but his assurances did nothing to ease Dan's memory of what had happened. He did not think it a bear. For one, it wasn't anywhere near heavy enough.

Dan retired soon after dinner tiring easily. Sitting alone in his room undressing carefully, wincing each time he turned against the bands of repairing muscle along his neck and back.

He also now felt uneasy over the Count's announcement that they needed another research student. He certainly didn't feel like going through all that again, even though it had thrilled him some the last time. How he could explain his feelings to the Count he did not know.

Later that night Anna came into his room and gently woke him. At first Dan though her to be just doing her nursing bit, something he had grown used to over the last few days, but when she let the heavy dressing gown she wore slip from his shoulders to the floor, Dan looked upon her nakedness, looking warm and inviting in the soft flickering light offered by the single candle which lit his room.

Carefully and slowly they made love, Dan stifling his cries and occasional discomfort as the tender flesh of his back and neck protested from his movements. Anastasia seemed even more aroused when he whimpered occasionally pulling away from him, teasing him, saying "Look at my body, Dan" touching herself with her long fingernails, repeating "Look at me, Dan" pushing his hands back to the bed as he reached up to caress her soft warm flesh "No, Dan, just look, it's just for you."

At that moment the Count burst in carrying a light. "So you ignore my advice concerning my sister, Dan."

Neither Dan nor Anastasia moved at first, then suddenly Anastasia became aware of her own nakedness standing over Dan's naked body on the bed. She grabbed for her dressing gown and ran to the door. The Count slapped her as she passed him shouting "I'll deal with you later whore sister." He then strode over to where Dan lay.

Reaching for the bedclothes to hide his embarrassment. Scared, he fumbled for the words to say to the Count but found none. As the Count reached him he didn't should as Dan expected but spoke softly.

"You have disappointed me, Dan, you gave me your word, you have abused the trust I had put in you, your soul must now be mine."

Dan said nothing he just lay not really understanding what the Count meant. He was frightened, more frightened than he had ever been. Every muscle had frozen to total immobility and that in itself added even more to his fear.

The Count now stood over Dan at his bedside. "Still, Dan, you may save me a lot of trouble by your actions, we can still work together, though not in the way you imagine."

The Count deftly produced a small syringe from somewhere within his clothing plunging it straight into Dan's exposed chest, sending Dan into a frightened drifting dream state, falling and falling, in a downward spiral of hopelessness and anguish, eventually settling into total blackness.

Chapter 6

A Stranger In The Village

⚜

THE TINY VILLAGE beyond Zyiec bore no name and was not represented on any map, it was simply referred to as the "Mountain Village" by locals. Not that this concerned the big man, who was clean shaven with closely cropped hair, as he made his way on foot up the winding rocky road leading upward towards the village. Carrying a large back pack and a Polish phrase book, with the latter being more of a burden than the heavy pack. He was fluent in English and French, his native tongues, but with Polish he struggled as he had only been studying it for a couple of months since he had decided to come to these mountains claiming to be a writer wanting to spend time isolated in a country community for background research for his next book.

As the sun was going down the stranger decided to make camp for the night on some level ground just off the road and he knew he wouldn't make it to the village before midnight.

He set out the small one man tent he carried in his pack and cooked a tin of stew on his camping gas stove, then lay back in his tiny tent. Sipping from a quarter bottle of whiskey, relaxing and listening to the night sounds though he wouldn't drink enough for his senses to dim too much. He knew what it meant to be alert, after all this wasn't an English woodland, here there were animals that could be dangerous. It wouldn't do to be too complacent. The revolver in his pocket helped calm his worries even if his memories still haunted him.

He slept fitfully waking at dawn. After boiling some water and making a cup of hot black coffee he packed up his things and set off uphill towards the village.

As he made his way along the road he watched the mists slowly clearing on the mountains, listening to the birds chirping and early morning animals scampering to life as the crunch of his boots on the road disturbed them.

It was late afternoon by the time he reached the edge of the village, people we were about their daily chores eyed him cautiously. Finding his way to the centre of the village he tried several times to communicate with the passers-by but they seemed far too wary of him to want to stop to talk, plus his Polish was very poor.

He stopped and took off his pack to rest outside the only building in the village that didn't look like the rest. He presumed that this must be the meeting hall come tavern, as it was by far the largest dwelling type building there. the majority of the other structures all looked like small cottages with two or three barn type buildings scattered around the tiny village.

After fifteen minutes or so a short portly man came out of the large building and walked straight over to where the stranger sat on his pack. The portly gentleman's conversation was lost on him. He spoke far too quickly for him to take any part in it, so he tried a little English. It was to no avail so he tried a little French which seemed to spark a little recognition.

The portly gentleman sent a young boy running off down the village path soon to return with a middle aged woman whose head barely came level with the stranger's chest. A few words were exchanged between her and the portly gentleman then she spoke in fluent French to the stranger.

He introduced himself as Keith Baker and told her of his being a writer, whereupon he asked if there was anywhere in the village he might find lodgings and somewhere to get a meal. She spoke again to the portly gentleman before informing Mr Baker that August in the tavern would provide him with food and drink but there was nowhere with lodgings to offer in the village. She explained they never get visitors here as the village is far too remote. As he presumed August was the portly gentleman. They followed him into the tavern, more of a meeting hall cum church, with a small bar set in front of a dozen stacked wooden kegs.

Keith Baker invited the lady to join him for his meal and she accepted his invitation to sit with him but would not eat with him. As she took a seat opposite she introduced herself as Eva Plachette, explaining that her late husband had been French. When he died some years ago she had returned here to the village where she had grown up. Having no children to occupy her time she lived her life out in the quiet loneliness of her sorrow and what quieter place than this.

As the afternoon turned to evening Baker asked if he could not find lodgings would August permit him to pitch his small tent on the patch of grass alongside the tavern. This resulted in rather heated discussion between Eva and August.

"Mr Baker." Eva turned to him her face flushed red with temper.

"Our good landlord will permit you to camp outside but are you aware of the dangers in these mountains? We have many wild animals around living in the woods and peaks. They would not normally wander into the village, at least by day, but we have had some livestock taken by night in these past few weeks. The villagers tend not to stray far after dusk."

Baker looked Eva in the eye, pleased that she did not avert her gaze as many people do but looked him squarely with her deep brown eyes, as if willing him to speak to her of things not spoken between strangers.

"Eva, I am very grateful for your assistance and your company, but do not worry, I shall be fine in the tent outside, after all I spent last night on the way up her in it and I am still here today."

"No, Mr Baker, the people here will talk but let them. if needs must you can stay at my cottage. i have no bed to offer you but the floor in my lounge is no harder than August's lawn, you will at least be safe from predators for the night before you move on tomorrow."

They shared a drink or two before Baker paid August and everyone in the tavern watched as Eva led him out and down the path towards her home, all talking in guarded whispers until the door closed behind them. Some even going to the windows to watch them walk down together.

They sat talking until late. Eva finding she felt at ease with Baker. She sensed he was a hard man but deep inside him was a naive sensativity, almost feeling him a kindred spirit in her loneliness. He was a man with secrets he would only share when he was ready to. The cottage was small and plain, a living room with two chairs and an open fireplace with a few homely knick-knacks placed on shelves here and there, polished wood floors with hand woven rugs scattered about. One small bedroom, a washroom without plumbing, water had to be heated on the iron range in the small kitchen, being first hand pumped at the stone kitchen wash stand.

Eva made a bed up for Baker on the lounge floor in front of the open fire, stacking a few extra logs on to keep from the evening chill and bidding him goodnight she then shut herself in her bedroom.

At breakfast Baker casually asked Eva about the castle and its occupants.

"A strange one that Count." Eva spoke guardedly as if someone were listening in. "Keeps himself pretty much to himself. I've seen his sister and a young man out riding some mornings but they don't often come near the village. Some of the old folks say that the Count's family is cursed. Some of them have never left the village all their lives, our country is steeped in folklore and the older folks still believe in many of the ancient tales."

"It is something I have studied myself, in fact that is the very subject I plan to write about."

Eva looked a little surprised when Baker told her and cautioned him not to pry too closely into the Count's affairs. "He is a powerful and jealous man and I believe does not take kindly to people asking questions, be careful Keith."

As Eva spoke to him she reached over and clasped his hand gently squeezing in an effort to persuade him of her sincerity and concern for his possible safety.

At that moment there was a knock on the door of Eva's cottage. She opened it to find most of the men from the village gathered together with tools and weapons all looking very angry though a glimmer of fear showed in many a pair of eyes.

"Bring him out Eva, justice will be done."

August seemed to have taken the roll of spokesman. Eva retorted calmly. "I don't understand August what is all this about?"

"Last night, madam, livestock was taken and butchered, some say the wolves have returned, but amongst the wolf tracks we found a man's footprint," He paused "though not an ordinary man's" he paused again as if trying to add weight to his statement "the mark of the werewolf. Did this man here go out last night? Were you with him all night?"

Baker had come to the door, the men started shouting, he knew something was wrong from the raised voices but he could not understand the conversation. Eva quickly told Baker of their accusations.

"They suspect you carry the mark of the werewolf." Eva got angry with August, then "You shame me August, I spend a night making myself a new friend and because of your stupid superstitions and some livestock missing, you jump to ridiculous conclusions." She paused for a deep breath but continued before August could speak up.

"Fools, that's what you are, you men and that damned Count up in the mountains. Keith was with me all night and to hell what you all think of my virtue. He is a gentlemen, especially compared to you, you're a lot of frightened stupid, Ooh!, I don't know, leave us alone."

Eva turned, pushed Baker into the cottage and slammed the door. She had lied, of course, she had not spent the whole night with Keith Baker.

The crowd began to disperse with mutterings and grumblings amidst suggestions of setting up a watch for that night. Nobody was eager to volunteer though.

Eva and Baker sat while she told him of their accusations. Baker felt awkward after she had stood up for him. His instincts told him he owed her the truth he had told no one, the whole truth. He even doubted it himself sometimes and right now he doubted strongly his reasons for coming to this place.

"Eva, I have lived a lonely life isolated from other men even when in a crowded place. There could be more truth in these men's claims than you think, thought it was not I who was responsible for last night's killings. I am sorry to have deceived you. I am not Keith Baker and I am not writing a book. I came here to attempt to investigate my suspicions of Count Versipellis, that he is linked in some way to the legend of the werewolf, it is something I do for myself alone. A greater explanation I beg you not to ask." He took hold of Eva's hands gently as he spoke wondering if she would accept his apology.

"My real name is Keith Stubbs. I am, or was, a policeman. That is how I cam across the Count but now I feel I must leave you for I have brought trouble to you and you are far too kind a lady to deserve it."

There was a tear in the corner of Eva's eye, taking her hand from Stubb's she put her arms around his waist and pulled herself to him.

"Please, Keith, don't go just now, not now, not when I've just found you." Eva had started to sob gently finished speaking.

Stubbs didn't know what to say to her so he jut held her feeling guilty for bringing his troubles to such a sweet lady.

Eva left Stubb's embrace, walked over to the door and bolted it, then taking him by the hand led him to the bedroom where they made love for most of the morning.

By mid-day, their passions being spent, they simply lay together caressing. Softly breaking the silence, Eva spoke.

"Loup Garou, do they really exist, Keith? I mean surely not."

"There are many things we dismiss as not existing Eva, simply because we don't know enough about them." Stubbs paused then as if considering whether he should confide in Eva, spoke almost in a whisper. "I do have what your menfolk would call the mark of the werewolf." Stubbs sat up letting the bed sheet fall away from him.

Eva gave a stifled gasp "Oh! my God."

"It was a long time ago, Eva, myself and two others were attacked in the mountain in Quebec. I was the only one to survive. These scars were given to me by what I believe to be a werewolf that attacked us. I could only describe it as neither wolf, nor man, but both. You are the only living soul I have told this to. it has been a burden to me for many years, the first ten being the worst. You see at the time I believed myself to be infected by the bites though I no longer feel that way now."

What Stubbs neglected to tell Eva was that for the first nine years after his ordeal he carried a horrifying craving for human flesh. His fear of actually becoming one of the things that attacked them had kept him strong. He thought that coming to England would help, no longer out in the woodlands and mountains, England has no wild wolves.

At times before he left Canada he would hear them calling to him. Whether they did or it was just in his nightmares he could not tell.

He studied all the folklore and legends he could and found that it was once believed if a werewolf did not eat of human flesh for nine years then he could become normal again. Even now, fifteen years later, Stubbs found his memories mixing with dreams and nightmares, never completely sure which were which, what was reality and what was not.

His initial intention in coming to Poland was to find out once and for all the truth. Now he was beginning to feel not quite as sure as he had been as to whether he could accept or was even ready to accept the consequences of what the truth might hold.

"I can help you, Keith. I have a friend from the village who is a servant in the kitchens at the Count's castle."

"No Eva, you must not take any more risks for me, you have already done enough."

"Keith" Eva sounded firm "I will help you for I feel now you have given me reason to want to live again and to put my brooding and sorrow behind me."

That afternoon Eva and Keith went over to August's tavern where the village folk were holding a meeting. Eva spoke to them all offering to prove Keith's innocence of last night's killings by both being prepared to help stand watch that night in the presence of witnesses to prove that Keith was nothing more than a man.

The villagers took some persuading but eventually decided that they would stand watch in turns using the tavern as headquarters where Keith and Eva would remain all night in the presence of the respective men of the watch.

It was a long night's vigil with a dozen different villagers taking shifts to watch over Keith and the surrounding area of the village. Patrolling the pathways in groups of three.

By dawn all conceded that there must have been some other explanation and Keith's arrival on that day could for now be put down to coincidence.

Stubbs did not speak of the feelings he had experienced during the night. He had sensed the closeness and presence of something inherently evil in the dark hours although nothing had come within the boundary of the village.

When the final dawn watch returned Eva and Keith made their way back to the cottage for a few hours sleep.

They awoke just after mid-day, ate a light lunch and Eva gave Keith some clothes more in keeping with the style the villagers wore.

"These shouldn't draw too much attention your way."

Stubbs questioned Eva's remarks. "What do I need these for?" He seemed a little bemused.

Without saying anything Eva opened Stubbs' back pack and rummaged about until she found what she was looking for. Removing his passport she help up his photograph.

"Look, you wouldn't even recognise yourself from this likeness so I'm quite sure the Count could be forgiven for not recognising you seeing as the one brief meeting you have had you wore a full beard, long hear and English style clothes. Just remember no to speak English while we are there."

"What do you mean Eva, while we are there?"

Stubbs and Eva were still arguing over whether it was safe for her to go to the castle together. Stubbs had intended to go along at night and look around alone when there was a knock on the cottage door.

It was August and two of the other men from the village. They told Eva they were sending a delegation from the village to ask the Count for help in stopping these attacks.

Some of the older villagers were against asking help from the Count though the majority felt if he would hunt down the beasts responsible it was at least worth asking. After all he did not do much else for them.

Stubbs and Eva decided to go along with the delegation. It would be a perfect cover for him to slip away and get a look around the castle. He finally accepted Eva's presence would be helpful in that if she could contact her friend who worked in the kitchens, her knowledge of the castle could prove invaluable. The delegation was about twenty strong, Stubbs and Eva tried to stay as inconspicuous as possible.

They had all assembled in the main courtyard. Mishcow left them standing outside while he returned into the castle to inform the Count of their wishes to speak to him.

Stubbs had been distracted by the figure of Anastasia watching from a balcony. His years of policework and evaluating people in an instant gave him the feeling of despair as he looked into the face of the lady on the balcony. When her eyes caught his she flushed and turned away quickly disappearing into the building.

Stubbs turned to ask Eva who she was but to his surprise she was not there. "Damn the woman" he cursed under his breath. At that moment the Count appeared in the doorway and Stubbs realised his chance to slip away was lost, he simply kept his head down and tried to blend in with the crowd, hunching himself down so as not to draw attention to himself.

Eva peaked through the kitchen door and hissed to her friend. There were two others in the kitchen at the time though neither of the other two women knew Eva. "Val, can you spare a moment, I'm here with the villagers but I can't stay long." Eva's tone was guarded as if she did not want the others to overhear what she wished to say to Val.

Val, a slim plain looking girl of about twenty made her excuses to the others and slipped out into the yard behind the kitchens. Eva did not have the time to tell Val the whole story, but instead made arrangements to meet at Eva's cottage on Val's next day off which was two days hence. Eva insisted that Val tell nobody of their meeting then slipped back into the main courtyard waiting just out of sight until the Count and villagers were finished before making her way back into the throng of people, her absence being noticed only by Stubbs who had hear the villagers request put to the Count though he hadn't understood most of it.

He had begun to pick up bits and pieces of the conversations. The Count had agreed to their request for help and was to take out a delegation of ten men and his hounds at dawn tomorrow to see what they could track down. Stubbs was not included in the villagers' negotiations of which ten men would accompany the Count.

Chapter 7

DISCOVERY

❧❦❧

D AN HAD LOST all track of time as he lay on no more than a bed of straw in the dungeons. The only break in his solitude was once day, he presumed once a day, for no light came into the pitch black of his prison except when the food was pushed through an opening trap in the prison door. Even though no light penetrated the damp gloom for more than a few seconds. He tried to keep himself active but could not combat the feeling of hopelessness that grew within him.

On one occasion he had heard a terrifying cacopheny of yelps and howls as if hell itself had opened up and taken all the hounds kept in the catacombs into its pitiless burning caress. At that time Dan had been almost paralysed with fear wondering if whatever had caused those torture suffering would be coming for him.

The Count had been forced to destroy the most advanced pack of dogs as they became increasingly more difficult to control, fearing they were only a step away from the condition Jadwega had lapsed into before his escape. his work for now centred upon autopsies and testing the slaughtered hounds for discrepancies from his previous finds. He must have tested and examined thousands of samples of tissue and blood from the dogs under the electron microscope. He was tired and frustrated curing to himself

"Thirty generations of trials and tests and I know less than all before me." He decided to take some rest, angry with his failure despite his turning t modern sciences as well as the old ways.

He made his way upstairs, not bothering with his evening meal, wishing to avoid his sister's pitious constant pleading for him to tell her what he had done with her lover. "He simply left." the Count had told her more times than he cared to think of.

As the Count had risen from his workbench he had disturbed two racks of test tubes containing the dogs' blood samples. Wiping the spilt blood from the broken tubes into a tray he simply put it on the worktop intending to clean it up tomorrow.

In his room he got very drunk and retired without eating, eventually waking the next morning having fallen asleep fully dressed.

He washed and changed and made his way down to the laboratory neglecting breakfast, expecting to have a mess of dried congealed blood to clear up before starting his work proper.

At first he was confused when he saw a thin film of blood on the worktop and in the tray he had used to contain the spillage was still fluid. But it had been there over twelve hours ago, it should have dried up by now.

His first thought was that one of the dogs must have carried some form of haemophilia in its blood. Though all the tests he carried out on what little there was of the samples of mixed blood from the test tubes bore no resemblance to the characteristics of haemophilus the rod shaped bacteria were not present and the only unusual bacteria present proved to be motile rather than non-motile, meaning it had the ability to move of its own accord, the haemophilus bacteria does not have this ability. There were two types of unrecognisable bacteria present, one medium sized and the other very large, both seemed able to move spontaneously though slowly.

The Count's excitement grew feeling he was on to a profound discovery in his work. Piecing the broken test tubes he found the blood samples came from two different dogs, both had been at the forefront of dominating the pack of twelve. By the end of that week had what he wanted, a batch of samples of each of the bacteria separated and ready for further testing.

The Count first tested the bacteria on mice finding definite characteristics in each, both causing different reactions.

The mouse with the larger bacteria present became reclusive as if shying away from light, presumably more sensative while the other was more slowly affected by the smaller bacteria, it became increasingly more aggressive. Though both specimens underwent some form of tremors and coma similar to those Jadwega had suffered, neither seemed to be physically altered as he had been.

It soon became apparent that the more aggressive mouse would kill its own kind indiscriminately for no apparent reason leaving the bodies to rot but at the same time the reclusive specimen would live comfortably with its own kind, except that every day or so it would kill just one purely for sustenance, neglecting any other food provided. It had become dependent on the flesh of its own kind for its survival and would only kill enough to sustain its nutritional requirements.

He decided he had to know more, he needed two specimens who could tell him what they were feeling.

Dan watched the Count carefully when he opened his cell door carrying usually a pitch torch in one hand whilst warning Dan to stay calm and not try anything.

"I don't want to hurt you". The Count's tone was cold and empty of the friendship Dan had once thought existed.

"I want you to volunteer your help, you must understand I need you as my next research specimen."

Dan was stunned. "What . . . ? After what happened to Jadwega you want me to volunteer?" Dan could actually feel his heart beat increase.

The Count was beginning to make Dan feel scared, it was as if he was exuding pure evil. Once again the Count spoke to Dan in a cold chilling but relaxed tone.

"Dan, would you rather be just a corpse to feed to the dogs, or would you be part of our work again. I have made a great advance since your indiscretions."

Dan realised that pleading with the Count would make no difference to his plight but if he was to go along with him for now he may be able to find a way to escape, the more Dan thought about it the more he came to accept that anything would be better than rotting to death in this dungeon.

The Count left Dan promising that if he co-operated he would be moved to a more comfortable room. Sometime later the Count returned and upon Dan's acceptance of the Count's terms he was led to another cell not a great deal different to the last one, although this one at least had a cot style bed, a table with a single chair and was lit by two candles which were stood on the table along with basic writing materials.

A short time later the Count brought Dan a bowl of warm stew with some bread and a tankard of wine. When Dan had finished eating and drinking alone in his prison cell he couldn't shake the feeling of becoming a human lab rat. He moved from the table and sat on the edge of the bed, laying back drowsily he was asleep within seconds as the drugged wine worked its way into his system.

As Dan lay asleep the Count stood outside the bolted cell door peering through the grill in the door contemplating the next steps in his research. He turned and walked away along the labyrinth of the dungeon passageways returning to his laboratory.

Back inside the lab the Count set to work preparing a sample of serum he had made up containing the larger bacteria from his tests and after making careful notes of exactly what was contained in this preparation he filled a hypodermic needle with the serum and returned to Dan's cell.

Unbolting the cell door he found Dan sleeping heavily breathing in long deep restful breaths which he attributed to the drugged wine but also the marginally improved air flow in his new cell.

Leaning over Dan spectre like in the dim light of the tiny room the Count, upon finding an accommodating vein in Dan's arm, injected the full dose wiping away the spot of blood left as he extracted the needle. The Count then turned and left Dan with a glimmer of satisfaction creeping over his sinister expressions. Bolting the door as he left impatient to return the following morning to see if any reaction had taken place.

Dan's reaction to the Count's touch as he came through the door was similar to that of the mice in the laboratory, to bright light although not quite as acute. He also complained of having cramps and a great thirst.

"Dan I want you to document all that you feel for me. You have a pen and paper. While you slept last night I gave you a dose of a serum far more advanced that any I have ever used before. You may be interested to know that another specimen I have used the same serum on is still healthy so you need not worry of any reoccurrence of what happened to Jadwega."

The Count then turned and left before Dan had a chance to ask any questions. He simply lay back on his bed and sighed thinking of the strange turn of events that led him to such a fate for he now felt sure in his despair that there would be no escape for him, just a sad and slow agonising death.

Anna's cheek smarted, marked red from her brother's slap, she ran to her room bolting the door behind her. Crying she lay on her bed too frightened to think of what the Count would do to Dan in his jealous rage. She cursed how he controlled her life. Since their parents had died Manfred had treated her as his daughter rather than his sister. This she accepted easily at first seeing as he was so much older than her. Many times as she grew older and more mature she had begun to resent the control he constantly exercised over her.

As the days passed, in her despair Anna sought solitude. She wandered the long forgotten wings and towers of the castle. She even found rooms that in all her thirty years she had never seen. As a child she had playing in castle, roaming and exploring all over, never once thinking there were places she did not know of. Her parents would only ever let her outside the castle walls when accompanied by an entourage large enough to dispel any child's ideas of play, although from an early age she had loved to go out riding.

It was while she was wandering in the high towers that she came upon the room and discovered a pile of dusty cobwebbed books hidden behind a tapestry covered partition. Several of the books were bound in old decaying ribbon. As Anna examined them she realised they were her great-great-grandmother's diaries.

With the bundle of books tucked neatly under her arm Anna returned to her room and for the next three days did almost nothing but sit and read them. By the time she had finished the final entry, Anna had become fully aware of just how naive she had been concerning her father and her brother's actions all these years.

Her great-great-grandmother, Zoya, told in the diaries of trials and burnings in the village presided over by Count Mikhail Stanislaw

Versipellis IV, Anastasia's great-great grandfather. He was a hard ruler of the local people and although he treated his wife and family well he was to be obeyed at all times.

From her great-great-grandmother's writings Anna could only presume that she had known a lot more of his work and past times than he ever suspected. Many villagers were taken by Mikhail into the dungeons for petty crimes, some were never seen again. Villagers often whispered of black magic and witchcraft though none would speak of it aloud.

The diaries also told of screams and cries in the night and of some nights when Zola would sneak down into the dungeons by way of a secret passage hidden in one of the lower rooms in the old tower wing of the castle and secretly tend some of the hideous wounds her husband had inflicted on the poor wretches, some of whom would simply disappear without a trace between her visits.

One diary in particular made reference to the histories of the Versipellis family and its cursed taint of the blood. But also written was the need of keeping the bloodline pure, this being an emphatic command handed down from Count to Count. Any female in the family who should put the bloodline at risk by virtue of immorality should be cleansed and punished.

When Anna read that she shuddered realising that was why her brother treated her as he did, but not only that, what did he now intend for her as part of her cleansing after what had happened with Dan?

Dan she realised must be in the dungeons. She hadn't even known of them. Even playing in the castle as a child she had been totally unaware of their existence. She hid the diaries in her room and set out determined to find the passageways her great-great-grandmother had used and had written of.

It was not going to be easy. The old tower wing must have had dozens of rooms, at least she knew it was one of the rooms in the lower levels.

Every day for a week she visited the wing, having no luck at all. Some of the rooms were almost derelict, thick with dust and cobwebs. Anna did wonder why these weren't cleaned any more, but then Manfred had never been over generous when it came to paying for servants.

It was just before sunset when Anna turned to leave the room she had been exploring when the hem of her dress caught on the rough stone corner of an old open fireplace. She heard the material tear, but something else, a distinct click. Looking around the room she could see nothing, although there was a definite sudden chill in the air. She could see the swirling patterns as dust mites floated haphazardly on the air, lit by the shafts of dwindling sunlight fighting its way through the old stained windows.

Anna put out her hand as if trying to touch the air. Trying to feel which direction the chill was coming from she stopped directly in front of the fireplace. "There." She gave a little gasp, there was a panel behind the fireplace. Bending down she leaned over the old grate and pushed against the panel, it was stiff but it gage. She paused checking she could find the trigger before closing it. Now was not the time, her brother was probably about somewhere down there.

Chapter 8

THE HUNT

—◆—

T HE COUNT WAS furious. The last thing he wanted at this time was to have to appease the villagers. A few days hunting and bring in a few lone wolves or a couple of the huge wild boar that populated the more remote areas of dense woodland should prove enough to satisfy the villager's tempers and calm them down for a while and allow him to get on with his work, especially now that he was beginning to feel like he may be getting somewhere with his research.

"Oh! God" he cursed. Obliged by his status as Count it was his duty to the people from the village the honour their request for help in this matter, but inside he resented their intrusion upon his privacy. Deep down he felt nothing but contempt for these peasants.

Grudgingly, he accepted that to keep the community peaceful in his province he head to make the odd gesture to the local peoples' requests. Better that he be in control of their attempts at satisfying the fears of their superstitions than they themselves let local trivialities get out of hand and end up having higher levels of governing bodies stick their noses into the business of what the Count considered to be his jurisdiction. He had to get out and bring things into line quickly. Not only to satisfy the villagers but also for him to return to work as soon as possible.

An hour before dawn the ten men from the village met outside August's tavern and made their way up toward the castle, each on horseback though most were not exactly prime examples of horseflesh. Most were cart or wagon horses and only five actually wore saddles. Each man though carried a hunting rifle even if some were antiques. Two men carried old muzzle loaders with power and ball.

The sun was creeping into the sky hidden from view as yet by the mountains to the East.

When they arrived at the castle the Count had a pack of fifteen dogs gathered and waiting in the courtyard. None of the dogs in this pack had been used for the Count's experiments yet, he did not want any of the villagers suspecting anything if he used any of the dogs with heightened senses and after having to destroy one pack he felt a little safer himself.

Alongside the grey stallion was the bay mare Dan had first ridden, carrying two large packs strapped either side of her flanks containing food, blankets and ammunition plus several cookpots, knives and axes.

From a window high above the courtyard, Anastasia watched. She did not see the tall short haired man who had caught her eye the previous day. Something about him had disturbed her.

The Count mounted the grey and handing the reins of the pack horse to one of the villagers trotted out of the courtyard, surrounded by the dogs, followed by the villagers. They headed back towards the village for a few miles before turning off the road towards the lower hills and woodlands.

It was very rate these days to find wolves in the lower hill there were always a few wild boar about. With the possibility that a roaming pack of wolves had strayed down from the more isolated high forests then here was as good a place as any to try to pick up a scent. It would be getting colder in the mountains now and if these wolves ran with a man or even a werewolf, then they may attempt pickings in the village.

Although if there was a werewolf abroad the Count was sure he would have known of it. He did consider the possibility that it could have been Jadwega but he was not sure whether he was still alive. After all the condition he had been in before his escape was not indicative of longevity.

It was mid-day when the dogs caught a scent. They ran through woodlands and over streams setting a frantic pace, finally settling to a more steady run indicating a sure but distant quarry.

The villagers were continually struggling to keep up, their horses being no match for the dogs and the Count's grey. Gradually the pack led them through the woodlands turning in a wide circle back toward the mountains heading South East in the direction of the Tatras, the high peaks of the Carpathians lying along the Czechoslovakian border. If they got that far the horses would be of no use to them in that countryside and that would mean a much longer trip than the Count had wanted.

By evening they still headed in the same direction. The dogs and horses were tired and needed a good rest to say nothing of the men. The Count halted the dogs and had them tied to some trees, as were the horses. While a few of the villagers took the axes from the packs and cut wood for a camp fire others made preparations with the provisions the Count had brought for a meal. A simple stew of meat and vegetables eaten with some bread and washed down with hot coffee. Passing out the blankets they settled in for a cold night, taking turns in pairs to keep watch and attend the camp fire.

Nobody slept well except for the Count. Their superstitions combined with the night sounds, a steady hum from high up sounding almost like a motor running, simply the breeze in the upper branches of the trees. The scampering of night woodland creatures was enough to keep them all on edge and the presence of the Count made them all a little uneasy. A frighteningly hard man, aloof and uncommunicative, leading them but not with them, although each and every one felt a lot safer with him there than they would have without him.

The night passed without incident. It was while they ate breakfast that one of the villagers mentioned to the Count the stranger they had first suspected of being a werewolf.

"A Frenchman, my Lord, but we checked him out and found him to be no more than he claimed. A writer travelling in the mountains." Sigismund had been quite pleased with himself and the simple fact that the Count had been interested in his conversation.

They set off again heading South East until the dogs picked up the scent again. A few hours later they came to a dense part of the forest. The dogs were acting more frantic, an indication they were getting closer but the horses would not be able to get through these dense woods.

Setting up a camp two men were left behind to tend the horses. The other eight villagers struggled to keep up with the Count and his dogs travelling at a steady run, each carrying their own guns and a small pack with a little food and a couple of axes shared out amongst the men.

The Count led with the dogs and the men spread out at ten foot intervals just close enough not to lose sight of each other.

As they ran they were constantly tripping and getting snagged by brush against their clothes, nobody escaped the cuts and scratches from the branches and thorns. Suddenly they burst from the forest, the dogs and the Count had come to a dead stop. Stretching out before them was the shore line of a small lake reaching to the base of steeply climbing rugged mountains.

The villagers sank to the ground gasping for breath thankful for the rest. The Count announced that whatever it was the dogs had followed had either sum into the lake or backtracked around them and nothing was visible on the lake, its surface almost like a mirror.

After resting a while and eating a little of the food each carried it was decided that they should return to the horses where they would consider what to do next. Several even suggested giving up the chase and heading for home. Most of the men had lost heart in the hunt weary from the hard pace the Count had set.

Bravely chatting and boasting about what they would have done if they'd found anything they made their way back through the forest at a much easier pace than they had set coming, with the exception of the Count that is. With the dogs still loose he was soon far ahead, the pathway left by the pack and the Count passing through the brush was soon the only sign left to the villagers that they hd been with them, but they were too tired to be bothered to try to catch up.

Almost without warning there was a thundering crash through the trees, one of the villagers who was lagging behind complaining of being exhausted was seized and carried off by something so swift that nobody got a proper look at it.

His screams echoed through the forest. A few men tried to shoot at it but were afraid they might hit their comrade. They did fire a few shots into the air as a warning to the Count that something was happening. They then tried to follow in the direction the beast had fled.

The trail of blood was not hard to follow, the forest was starting to thin as they made their way nervously forward, trees eventually giving way to a clearing of not more than five yards before becoming a rocky cliff face dotted with caves rising steeply skyward. The trail of blood led straight into one of the caves.

Each man looked uncertainly to his fellow. Nobody was eager to volunteer to go into the cave.

"Maybe we should wait for the Count." Sigismund suggested. They all agreed with Sigismund then fired off a couple of shots to indicate their location to the Count who they hoped was rapidly approaching with the dogs. They all stood around nervously waiting for them to arrive.

When the Count did arrive with the dogs at the cliff face, the villagers practically fell over each other in an effort to be the one to give the news of events to the Count.

When they had garbled out the general story to him the Count instructed them to first cut some wood and make up some torches. They kept the dogs close as the Count and three of the villagers entered the case bearing the bloody trail. Each carrying a burning torch and each balancing his rifle ready for use at a moments notice. The four remaining men took up positions outside the caves and waited ready to pick off any creatures other than man or dog which tried to escape the darkened caves.

Once inside the cave the men had to stoop to avoid cracking their heads on the ceiling it was so low. The torches cast eerie dancing shadows all around and the smoke they gave off blew straight back into their faces making their eyes sting. Even the Count moved with great caution now.

The growls and panting of the dogs made it difficult to listen for impending danger as the sounds echoed bouncing off the damp craggy walls of the cave heightening the sense that something was lying in wait for them just out of sight.

The dogs suddenly went berserk and raced into the blackness ahead. For the first time the Count lost his dominant control over his dogs and from the unseen depths of the tunnels ahead came a cacophony of growls, barks and howling. The dogs had something caught and it was putting up quite a fight.

The men followed the Count forward torches held in shaking hands grasping their guns tightly ready to shoot at anything coming their way. Nobody had time to react quickly enough to get a shot off at any of the animals as they burst into view.

Bloodstained, grey fur bristling, hackles up with eyes like fire reflecting in the yellow torchlight seen only for a split second before tearing past the stunned villagers who were not even aware how many wolves had just raced passed hotly pursued by the pack of equally bloodied dogs frantically trying to bring down the fleeing wolves.

Shots rang out killing half a dozen of the wolves as then ten of them raced from the cave into the daylight. The four waiting villagers being ready having heard the commotion emanating from the cave. They had positioned themselves at the edge of the treeline to give time and a little cover from whatever it was that was definitely heading their way. The three men inside the cave with the Count turned to follow the dogs out when the Count stopped them saying there may be some more animals left in the cave and reminding them of their lost friend. In their fright they had forgotten him.

They pressed on deeper into the cave. it opened into a larger cavern, at one end they could see some shadows, towards the centre lay several shapes making small whimpering sounds. Four of the Count's dogs were dead, torn to pieces, two wolves also lay dead.

A growl came from the end of the cavern where there were the other shadows, cautiously all four men approached. Slumped behind three covering injured wolves was a human figure. The wolves although badly mutilated by the dogs crouched defensively. The frightened villagers wasted no time, they raised their rifles and shot the three wolves who then convulsed and died before the echoes of the gunfire faded in the cavern.

The floor was awash with warm sticky blood as they made their way forward towards what they presumed to be their savaged comrade thinking the wolves had simply been protecting their food source, but as they drew nearer it was clear that they were walking through bloody mess of flesh and entrails that was once their friend and companion.

The man now cowering before them filled them with horror and revulsion. He was almost naked but for an old filthy and tattered pair of pants, his feet were bare but what made the villagers gasp was the look of his skin and face. His body was covered in scars and the skin looked like hard dark leather. His face was a mask of the same leather stretched over a bony skull. His hair was filthy and matter, but worst of all his eyes and teeth.

He looked nervously from face to face of the four men that now approached him pulling himself back as if trying to disappear through the hard stone wall. The last face he looked upon was the Count's, his eyes widened in terror.

The bullet from the Count's rifle passed straight through his forehead startling the already shocked villagers.

"There, you have your werewolf" the Count spoke caustically "Nothing more than a madman living wild with these animals."

Once the villagers had got over their shock they picked up Jadwega's body and dragged it out of the cave to show the other men. The villagers wanted to carry the body back to the village to show everyone there, but the Count argued that it would be easier simply to burn it here with the rest of the dead animals.

This time the Count was overruled, the men insisted that everybody in the village would feel safer knowing of the destruction of this creature, witnessing it burn with their own eyes. Two men made up a litter to carry the body on while the others set about burning the bodies of the dead animals.

Only four of the Count's dogs had returned by the time they started to make their way back to where the horses were. It was way past dark when they met up with the men waiting around the camp tending the horses. When they saw the men approaching they immediately set about making a meal.

The night's conversation was taken up entirely with the tale of the hunt, growing in stature every time it was told. The dogs were restless which in turn set the men's nerves on edge, the presence of Jadwega's body in the camp served only to heighten the nervousness of the men.

Every woodland sound seemed to trigger a reaction washing through each of the sleepless men. On more than one occasion the Count had tried to passify them saying it was probably just a boar rummaging in the nearby undergrowth and would not approach the campsite with a good fire burning. They all made sure the fire was well stocked.

They breakfasted early and tied the body on to the back of their dead companion's horse and set off for home.

The ride was uneventful and by dusk they approached the edge of the village where a crowd soon gathered to greet the returning hunters.

Quite a few of the women let out stifled screams and gasps as they gazed upon Jadwega's body. The Count watched but he made no comment casually trying to see if he could spot the stranger Sigismund had told him of. He was not difficult to find. A big man with close cropped hair and clean shaven. The Count didn't recognise him for who he was but there was a spark of something familiar about the man. He told the villagers to build a fire and burn the creature they had brought back with them.

"It will put an end to your superstitions." He then added that he was leaving to return to the castle. As he turned he told them they may return the blankets and packs he had supplied them with the following day. Mounting his grey stallion he rode off into the night.

The whole village watched the blaze from the fire and celebrated their success although they took time in silence to remember the one man lost to them who had given up his life for their safety. August had brought out a keg of wine and a tray of tankards, everybody drank freely until the fire embers were just a deep red glow. The hunters telling their stories over and over, improving on each telling until the last of the people gathered had retired for the night.

Chapter 9

ESCAPE

❧❦❧

AS SOON AS Anastasia saw her brother leave the castle on the hunt with the villagers she set about finding the way from the trap door behind the fireplace in the tower wing to the dungeons where she suspected Dan was still. She dressed in boots, trousers and a blouse similar to what she wore when riding, and carried an oil lamp with her.

Once she had reached the room with the secret passage she lit the lamp then triggered the release on the fireplace. Crouching down she squeezed through the opening, it groaned against its hinges as she leaned her weight against it. Ahead of her was a very narrow passage with tight corners winding its way downward, thick with cobwebs. The air in the passageway was heavy with dust as her movements disturbed the air.

Eventually she reached a solid stone wall. Fortunately on this side of the wall there was an iron lever set at shoulder height. Anna stood still for minutes listening intently wondering what was on the other side of the wall. All she could hear was the sound of her own breathing.

Hesitantly she pulled on the lever, a panel in the wall grudgingly swung open. Anna stepped into the damp corridors of the catacombs. The lamplight reflecting off the rough surface of the walls and ceiling.

The glow from the light carried for about ten paces in any direction. "Which way to turn" Anna though worried that if she got lost she may never find her way out again.

Sounds occasionally assailed her ears, eerie moaning growls. She was terrified and wondered whether she should return to the upper levels of the castle not coming back down until she had armed herself.

"Maybe it's just the wind" she tried to convince herself. Biting her lip she took a deep breath and turned to the left of the passage, keeping to the centre she strode forward fighting her fears every step.

The sounds began to take on more than just imagined rumblings of breeze in the tunnels. Anna cam to two doors opposite each other in the corridor. She peered in one through the barred opening in it. It was empty. She then looked through the opposite door. Even before she looked through, the stench assailed her delicate nostrils. The little light the lamp put out through the grill in the door was enough to make her turn away and balk.

As the dim glow of the oil lamp spread over the room the floor seemed to move. Anna instantly realised it wasn't the floor moving but a sea of rats feeding on a mass of foul smelling rotting flesh and bones, though it was impossible to tell from what creatures these remains had come from. Steeling herself she moved on.

By now she was starting to make out the occasional bark of a dog, realising her brother must keep more of his precious hounds down here. She worried and prayed that they would be locked up behind the walls of the dungeons and not roaming free somewhere in the darkness ahead.

She told herself "If I don't find something soon, I'm turning back." Already she had lost track of how far she had come.

The next doorway she came to she could hear the sounds she had partly expected and with some relief she realised that the door was locked. Peering through the grill she was greeted by two dozen yellow staring eyes causing her stomach to know, hoping they would not start making a noise. She could not understand why her brother would keep so many of his hounds down here and not next to the stables with the other dogs, which he had taken with him early that morning.

From there her confidence grew, satisfied in the knowledge that all the dogs were locked away. The creators of the growls and moans that haunted her in the dark were locked away and could not confront her in the dim passageways.

She came across three more chambers with dogs inside. Each time the animals seemed less interested in her presence than the previous packs had.

Then she noticed light emanating from around the curve of the passageways, moving to the left side of the tunnel she placed the lamp on the floor and moved as quietly as she could along the wall towards the distant light. Slowly the light grew brighter, a row of pitch torches stood in brackets on the walls at intervals close enough to light the whole passageway as it curved out of sight.

Anna stopped, keeping herself flat against the wall listening to the sound of her own breath. She almost believed it should have echoed in the tunnels it seemed so loud to her. Frightened she inched her way forward into the light.

As each day passed, Dan found himself becoming more and more alert to things he would never have even noticed before. His eyesight had altered, he could see well even in the dimmest of light. He knew whether it was the Count or Mishcow who brought his meals well before they arrived simply by the approach of their smell, he could easily tell the difference. His hearing improved also although there wasn't much to listen to in the dungeons other than the dogs or again when the Count or Mishcow approached, aside from the scurrying of rodents and insects. He was restlessly pacing up and down in his cell, aware of Mishcow's presence in the catacombs though he could tell he wasn't too close. "Probably seeing to the dogs" he thought.

At that moment he caught a trace of a new scent to him, a mix of two main smells, one sweet and musky and the other sweetly pungent as if laid over the other to mask it. Dan moved instantly to the door and peered through the grill. All he could see was the torch lit walls of the catacombs curving away in either direction.

The scent Dan had noticed seemed to be emanating from the opposite direction to that of Mishcow's scent. Slowly it grew stronger, the Dan's sharp ears picked up the slow careful footfalls of somebody approaching stealthily. His heartbeat quickened with the adrenalin surge the curiosity and anticipation brought to him.

"Anna" Dan whispered, stretching his hand through the grill of his door as he sensed her approach. She jumped backwards in surprise stifling an audible gasp. Quickly steadying herself she came up to the door. "Dan, what has Manfred done to you?"

"Shush Anna, Mishcow is about somewhere down here." Dan's voice was quiet and guarded. Had Anna known about his being imprisoned by the Count and if so why had she waited so long before coming to see him. He then remembered just how little the Count had said she knew of his work and also the way she had approached his cell. He guessed that she had only recently found out.

"Help me, Anna, I've got to get away from here, he's filling me with all kinds of potions and drugs. He will kill me with his experiments, I've got to escape soon, please, please, help me."

Anna drew back the bolts of Dan's cell door. To him it sounded like a rifle shot, the door swung open and Dan stepped into the light. His feet bar, his shirt and pants thick with dirt, Anna noticed that he did not smell too good either.

"Hurry, this way." She whispered.

They headed straight for the passageway picking up the oil lamp on the way. Anna chewed at her bottom lip anxiously hoping all the time that the doorway to the secret passage had not closed on itself barring their escape. More than once Anna felt that they must have gone past where the doorway had been. She heaved a sigh of relief when it came into view. Pushing Dan through the small opening she followed into the narrow passageway, pulling the secret panel closed behind her. She only then put her arms around Dan and hugged him.

"Oh! Dan, I would have come sooner if I'd known."

Dan was elated and hugged Anna back just as tightly, pleased he had guessed right about her.

"No Dan, we must get out of her quickly." Anna prised herself from Dan's embrace and led the way back up towards the tower wing of the castle, at the same time trying to form a plan of escape in her mind.

"We must get you out of the castle before Manfred returns. I don't know how long he will be away, but I don't suspect it will be very long."

When they stepped into the room from the passageway Dan had to cover his eyes, they were so sensitive that the daylight streaming through the window almost blinded him.

"A few minutes to adjust, I'll be OK" he assured Anna. She took him by the hand and led him through the corridors of the castle until they were safely locked in Anna's bedroom. Dan's eyes were beginning to adjust to the brightness now though still he squinted hard.

"You wait here Dan, and lock the door. I am going to get some transport for us. I think some of the servants are going down to the village this afternoon. I'll go and find out what is happening."

Val looked up surprised when the Lady Anastasia walked into her quarters dressed in riding gear and covered from head to foot in dust and cobwebs.

"My Lady!" was all Val could think to say.

"Valerie, it is your day off today, is it not?"

"Yes, my Lady, I was about to go into the village to visit some friends, but if it is inconvenient I can . . . ." before Val had finished Anna stopped her. Putting a hand on Val's shoulder Anna spoke to her softly. "It is very convenient." Anna paused for just a few seconds as if trying to add weight to her next statement.

"May I trust you with a secret, Valerie?"

"Why, yes my Lady." Val instantly wondered if whatever was going on had anything to do with why Eva wanted to see her. Only one way to find out, she thought to herself.

Anna spoke now more guardedly. "You must tell nobody, especially my brother or Mishcow. Now how are you travelling to the village?"

"I have a small horse and buggy ready, my Lady, I was just about the leave."

Anna arranged with Val for her to leave fifteen minutes later and told her to stop the buggy and wait twenty years past the bend in the road out of sight of the castle gateway. Val agreed wanting to ask why but giving way to a little patience and diplomacy.

Anna clasped Val's hands in her own and gave them a short squeeze, whether to reassure herself or Val she wasn't sure. She then turned and hurried back to her room, cautiously avoiding any of the other servants.

Anna and Dan made their way to one of the entertaining halls in the west wing of the castle. She chose this room in particular because it had a set of bay windows overlooking the western woodlands. They both crossed the room to the bay where Anna unlatched one of the windows. It was a good ten foot drop from the window to a steeply sloped grassy bank. Lowering himself to arms length over the window ledge Dan dropped and rolled down the bank, followed immediately by Anna, both coming to a rest at the bottom of the slope, ruffled but uninjured.

Climbing to their feet they ran quickly to get out of sight of the castle and headed towards their meeting place with Val. All the time Anna worried if Val would keep her word. She didn't know the girl well but liked her and thought her to be a genuine person, hard working and honest. She always seemed cheerful and that was what made Anna like her more than most of the other servants.

Relief surged through Anna as she spotted the buggy with its rainhood up as she had asked Val to do. Val's eyes were wide with shock when Dan climbed in followed by Anna.

"Let's go." Anna wheezed, her breath ragged from running. Dan huddled down between the two women still too stunned to think clearly, being both anxious and relieved at the same time. It was some time before he managed to speak. They set off, Val driving the horse and buggy at a steady pace so as not to draw attention.

"Whwhere are we going?" Dan stammered shakily. Anna looked at Val before speaking.

"Valerie has a friend in the village she thinks will help."

"She's a good friend and we can trust her, it should be okay." Val added.

It was the first time Dan had heard Val speak. He had, of course, previously seen her about her duties in the castle but was now touched by the softness and care in her tone.

Anastasia told Val that she would see that anybody who helped them would be well rewarded. Little more was said as the trio trotted towards the little village.

Anna and Dan sat back in the buggy trying to stay out of sight of the people's coming and goings in the village as they waited while Val disappeared into Eva's cottage.

Eva introduced Val to Stubbs though she used the name Keith Baker as he had used on his arrival in the village.

"Eva, I must talk privately, it's rather a difficult matter."

Eva assured Val that it was okay to talk in front of Keith and added that he couldn't understand a word of Polish, then added that even if he could understand it was alright to talk freely. Val told Eva the tale of Anna's plea for their help speaking of some trouble involving the Count and Anastasia then asked Eva's forgiveness in case she had done the wrong thing by bringing them here.

"No, no bring them in quickly, whatever is going on I think it is linked together. Now hurry."

Val went outside to the buggy and ushered Dan and Anna into the cottage. Quickly shutting the door behind them she commented that she did not think anyone about had noticed.

Eva quickly told Keith some of what Val had said and he commented that he was sure that it was inked to what he suspected the Count was up to. Then added that they must be careful because if he was correct they were taking some very great risks.

When they entered the cottage Stubbs instantly recognised Dan despite the beard, but said nothing. He simply nodded, hello. Eva, Val and Anna chatted on in Polish for quite some time then Eva turned to Keith, and Anna turned to Dan explaining what they thought best, Eva in French and Anna in English.

What they decided was that Anna and Val would return to the castle and both could make out they knew nothing of Dan ever having even been there. In the course of the next few days Anna would find some pretext on which to travel to the city and arrange for the withdrawal of a substantial sum of money and she and Dan would simply leave the Count to his castle in solitude and find somewhere they could set up a comfortable home together.

Stubbs said nothing, he simply went along with what they had planned.

Anastasia and Val left the cottage soon after and returned to the castle. Anna managed to slip back to her bedroom unnoticed and Val gave an excuse as to why she had returned so early, her friend was poorly.

Later Anna noticed that Mishcow as disturbed by something though as was his place he spoke not of it.

"Well, you could do with a wash and some clean clothes, Dan." Stubbs declared. Dan was startled when he was spoken to in English. "You look like you could do with a little rest too" he added. Dan could only agree on all three counts.

The jumper and pants Keith gave Dan were a couple of sizes too large but once he was cleaned up and in clean clothes Dan sat in the living room cradling a hot mug of coffee and began to relax a little.

Stubbs thought it safer to stick to his story of being a writer of folklore and interested by rumours of the reclusive Count Versipellis to justify his presence there.

He also thought Dan might confide little more in him that way he certainly didn't think the knowledge of who he really was would make Dan feel any easier and although this was the man who had caused him all this trouble, a man he was supposed to arrest as a possible murder suspect, he quite liked him on his first impressions. It seemed to Stubbs that Dan had been through quite a lot.

Dan talked to Stubbs about his ordeal in the dungeons and that the Count had injected him on three different occasions with a serum, the effects of which he was told to document. He was hesitant to give Stubbs all the details about why he was at the castle so told him he was a guest of Anastasia's rather than the Count's which seemed plausible because of the reason for his imprisonment at the hand of the Count. Anger and jealousy directed at his sister's lover and giving him the excuse to acquire the research specimen he wanted.

To Dan, Stubbs was a good listener, it was helping his state of mind by having a sympathetic ear.

Eva came in with the evening meal, a great steaming bowl of rabbit stew. While Stubbs ate heartily Dan merely picked at his, not what Stubbs expected from a man who had been imprisoned getting simple rations for some time.

When questioned over his lack of appetite Dan simply excused his lack of appetite on his nerves being on edge. A perfectly reasonable excuse, but not true. Dan could not bear the taste of the cooked meat and vegetables, inside he was fighting his craving for fresh raw meat. In actual fact he was starving, but was too frightened to ask for raw meat.

Over the meal all three chatted courteously of Stubb's translations of French to English and vice versa.

Eva suggested that Dan and Anna should travel first to the city and then on. Anastasia was certainly wealthy enough for them to settle in another country somewhere far enough from her brother's control.

Dan explained that his problem with that plan was that he had no papers and couldn't possibly get through any borders. Eva asked if he could not get new papers from the British Embassy in the capital, saying his were lost or stolen. Dan did his best to avoid a direct answer but made up the excuse that all might not be too well with the authorities and himself, nothing too serious (he lied) but easier that they did not meet.

Eva was too polite to enquire further and Stubbs showed a lack of interest in anything other than Dan's experiences with the Count.

He was sure he would get Dan's story of what had happened in England when he had more of his trust and for that he first had to help him over his ordeal at the castle.

In the back of Keith Stubb's mind was also the possibility that Dan might prove very useful in helping him find out more of his suspicions about the Count's real motives for all this research and seclusion.

The more he thought of it the greater his memories of fifteen years ago weighed upon his soul. He felt even if the Count was not personally responsible, if he was right his kind were, and he had vowed then to see them destroyed. Yes, he believed in werewolves alright though Eva was the only person in those fifteen years he had ever spoken of it to. He wondered if he was getting old and his resolve was weakening, or was he really just plain old scared that he may be right about the Count.

Dan spent that night on the living room floor in front of the fire disturbed by dreams difficult to separate from real memories. Each time he woke he would stare at his hands in the flickering glow of the fire, examining every detail to see if they had altered in any way. He remembered only too well the appearance of Jadwega's skin under the Count's treatment and was all too aware of the change in his senses. He was also worried about how much he should trust this Keith Baker and even Anastasia for that matter, after all she was the Count's sister.

Any why should Baker turn up here now writing a book on folklore and werewolves, something of a timely coincidence. Dan resolved to ask more of Baker tomorrow, after all he had asked enough questions of Dan, why shouldn't he answer a few as well?

As Eva gave both men their breakfast, Dan so hungry he put up with the foul taste of the bread, the bacon was more to his taste albeit overcooked.

All through the meal Dan intended to engage Baker in conversation but could not think of how to broach the subject, everything sounded so far fetched when spoken of, but neither man could deny what was happening around and to them.

After Eva had cleared the breakfast things she went out for a while, returning with some clothes borrowed from another friend on some pretext she had made up. These were a much better fit for Dan and he felt a lot more comfortable in them.

The rest of the day was spent waiting about for Anastasia's return, by dusk they concluded she was not coming this day.

If she did not arrive by mid-day tomorrow, it was decided that Eva would go up to the castle and meet with Val to see what she could find out.

They were ready to turn in for the night when Dan said he could hear something, minutes later the village burst into a cacophony of yells and shouts as the hunters and the Count rode into the village.

Everybody was outside to greet them, Eva and Stubbs also went out, nothing would have stopped Stubbs from watching this spectacle. Doing his best to get as good a look as possible at Jadwega without drawing too much attention to himself. That notwithstanding he noticed the Count's interest in him before he trotted off towards the castle, dogs in tow.

Dan's stomach turned and guilt swept through him as he watched what they did to the sorry creature they had brought into the village to burn. He could not help thinking, was it him who really attacked me in the woods, if it was it was probably what he deserves anyway.

Dan cursed himself for ever letting himself be taken in by the Count, he regretted a lot of things lately.

Later on in the evening Dan and Stubbs were talking. Dan told him of the attack on him on the fringe of the woods that day, Stubb's comments on that surprised him.

"I very much doubt that sorry creature was responsible for that kind of attack. He didn't look strong enough to fight off one man let alone the dogs."

Chapter 10

FRENZY

❦

MISHCOW GREETED THE Count on his return, he looked pale and frightened the Count could not help notice. Sternly he asked "What is wrong Mishcow?"

"It's Dan, Sir, he is not in his cell. All the doors were locked but yesterday when I came down to feed the dogs the bolt on his cell was drawn and the door open. I am sorry, Sir."

The Count stormed inside shouting obscenities at Mishcow for his incompetence.

Up in her room Anna could hear him, frightened she crossed to her door and locked it. The servants were disturbed from their sleep by the noise, several of them rising expecting to be called upon by the Count on his return, thinking he would require a meal and bath.

Those servants did not include Val, she alone amongst them knew the reason for the Count's rage. Dressing she made her way through the dark halls to Anastasia/s room and timidly knocked on the door calling out. "My Lady, it is I, Valerie, please my Lady, may I see you?"

Anna opened the door and let Val in re-locking it behind her. "My Lady, the Count has returned, I fear he is in a terrible temper." Val's voice was trembling.

"Yes, Valerie, we must be calm and also careful. You must say nothing."

Seized by an uncontrollable rage, feeling as if he blood were beginning to boil forcing muscle tissue into agonising spasms. Pure hate and hunger burned through him, the clothes he wore ripped to shreds as the final throes of the metamorphosis took place.

This time it was out of control, usually he was prepared for the transformation, letting it happen only when he allowed it to, but not this time.

He paced the floor salivating excessively. Mishcow walked in through the door expecting a tongue lashing from the Count. What he saw paralysed him with fear. The great silver grey coat of a huge abomination, half crouched on the floor of the dining room, yellow blood shot eyes glaring right through him, neither man nor wolf, disproportionately shifting from all fours to hind legs, great slobs of saliva dripping on to the polished floor.

Before he knew what happened Mishcow was flattened, two huge sharp clawed forepaws pressing the air from his lungs as they pinned his chest to the floor. Hot rancid breath steaming into his face making him gag and his eyes water. Just before the great man of the beast closed over his face crushing his skull like eggshell Mishcow's last action was to lose all control over his bodily functions. After eating no more than the brain and the eyes, the beast moved on heading towards the servants' quarters.

Two women were lighting the stove in the kitchen when it came through the door. Their screams reverberated around the whole castle bringing others running to the kitchen in time to see the beast standing on its hind legs howling over the two headless women. The howls sent all in the castle into panic stricken fear.

All the castle staff ran towards the courtyard intending to flee the castle. Those who had caught sight of the beast were babbling incoherently pushing and shoving past each other in their fear, almost turning against friends simply to escape.

Anna and Val held each other, shaking. Anna pulled herself away and dressed quickly, blowing out the oil lamp. They crossed to the window and watched as the servants came spewing out of the doors and across the courtyard, then they saw the beast leap from the main castle entrance.

With each swipe of its giant paws bringing down bodies upon which it fed on the brains and eyes only. It appeared to take its time with its victims seemingly unconcerned about the people escaping as if it knew it would get them all in its own good time.

Seeing that the creature was outside the castle Anna opened her bedroom door and led Val towards the tower wing, lighting the lamp on the way. Terrified they both moved quickly, when they arrived at the room where Anna had found the secret passageway she triggered the trap door behind the fireplace scrambling through the opening with Val close behind, then closing the doorway tight shut.

"We should be safe here." Anna's voice did not sound as confident as she had meant it to.

"What was that thing?" Val wept though her words.

"I don't know for sure Valerie, but things I have found out recently." Anna paused stuck for words for a few seconds. "I'm not sure, but I'm scared do you believe in werewolves?"

"Oh! my God, is that what it was?" Val was getting hysterical, Anna slapped her.

"I'm sorry, Valerie, I think it might be but I'm not sure, please calm down. We will be safe here, we can go to the village in the morning but for now let's try to keep quiet."

The corridor seemed to close in on them as the night wore on. Both women huddled together on the floor drifting in and out of sleep, straining to listen to every little noise that stirred their darkened solitude.

As dawn broke Louis, the stable lad, reached the edge of the village exhausted and he fell against the door of August's tavern. Too weak to shout he lay in a heap gasping for breath until he summoned up the strength to bang on the door.

When August eventually opened it Louis babbled out the tale of horror and his flight from the castle not knowing if anyone else had survived. He had run across the country, most of the others had stuck to the road. He knew the countryside well as he was often out exercising the Count's horses.

August helped him in and gave him a mug of hot coffee in an effort to calm him down. He then made him repeat his story again slowly. Louis said he didn't know what the creature was but one glimpse of it was enough and the noises it made, the howling was enough to chill the bravest hunter to the bone.

August sent out his boy to fetch some of the villagers and within twenty minutes a dozen bleary-eyed men sat in the tavern listening to Louis repeat his tale again. When he had finished one man suggested they seek the Count's advice and help again but Louis interrupted. "Some of the servants claimed it was the Count before they died." Every man in the room was silent looking from one to another, then August spoke up.

"Well, it looks like it's up to us, I think we should muster every able-bodied man in the village and go up there. If this creature and the Count are one and the same we all know what must be done. Gather what weapons you have and bring torches, if necessary we will burn down the castle."

One or two of the men put up arguments like "What if it's still there?" and "What if it comes into the village while we are up at the castle?"

August spoke out "We must not be negative in this we have to rid ourselves of this curse once and for all. While we are gone the women folk can barricade themselves in their homes or in here and we can set fire traps before we leave. Now, let's get on with it. Go and pass the word to meet here in one hour. Every man available must do his share."

The word spread through the village like wildfire. When the knock came on Eva's door, Dan got up and hid in the kitchen while Eva opened the door. She instantly told Keith who, in turn, told Dan of the night's events. Dan's first thoughts were for Anastasia. Was she alright? Keith turned to Dan and said "We have to go with them."

Dan just stared back at him, he was not ashamed to admit he was scared stiff of meeting the Count again, let alone this creature. But the thought of revenge against the Count for what he had done to him for whatever this poisonous serum was doing to him made him angry though to try to overcome his fear.

By mid-day the firetraps were set, the women were huddled into two groups spread between one of the large cottages and August's tavern, with the exception of Eva. She insisted on going with the men so as to translate for Keith.

The villagers eyed Dan suspiciously. Eva told them straight he had been held by the Count as a prisoner and tortured for his involvement with Anastasia. She also pushed the point that his knowledge of the castle would be invaluable. Reluctantly, they agreed.

Sixty men spread between three carts set off up towards the castle. Stubbs carried his .38 revolver, some of the others carried rifles. There were a couple of shotguns but most made do with scythes, knives and axes. It was agreed that those with guns should take the front line when they arrived.

On the road they found what was left of the servants' bodies, headless and looking as if scavenging birds and animals had fed well on the corpses, so much so that no one could tell who was who.

The sight of these enraged the villagers, spurring them on towards the castle, not bothering to stop to bury what was left of the corpses.

Everybody in the carts were nervous as they approached the castle. It was late afternoon when they faced the entrance to the courtyard. The castle entrance stood ominously open like a giant mouth waiting to swallow all who entered. There was not a sound to be heard.

Dan Stubbs and Eva took the lead of half the men heading towards the open door while the rest of them skirted round the grounds.

The pungent smell of death assailed Dan's sensitive senses, also strong was the Count's scent confusing Dan's attempts to locate him with his heightened sensitivities.

Cautiously searching the ground floor first they found what was left of Mishcow and the other servants. What little was left of them was enough to turn the strongest of stomachs. Stubbs had to keep reassuring Eva.

From room to room, some men waiting outside while the rest checked the room. Stubbs, Dan and Eva always in the lead. None of the village men being keen to turn the next corner or open the next door. The line of men had to thin out to move down the tiled corridors, those bringing up the rear feeling fidgety and nervous.

It was impossible for that many men to move through the castle quietly so many boots on the tiles created quite a racket forewarning anyone of their approach.

The group outside having much the same trouble except for the confinement of the castle corridors. August led this group, double barrelled shot gun gripped firmly in his hands, every man's eyes searching for movement in the shadows and alcoves of the architecture of the castle and its surrounding walls.

August told the men to spread out, otherwise if anything happens we will end up shooting each other. Hesitantly the men thinned out over the grounds settling into six groups of five, each group watching the other so as not to stray too far from each other, timidly trying doors, most of which being locked.

When someone found a door open everybody watched and waited as the five checked the room immediately through the door.

August pushed the kitchen door, it moved, then something blocked it. August jumped back drawing every man's attention. At first he thought someone had pushed against the door when he had started to open it, but when he jumped back the door stayed ajar.

The men gathered around, weapons ready, August plucked up his courage, leaning heavily against the door it gave. Pushing the bloodied faceless corpse across the sticky red stained kitchen floor all five men fought to hold on to the contents of their stomachs. Stepping through the congealed blood on the floor they checked the kitchen, empty except for the corpse. As they made their way out each man avoided looking upon it again.

Back inside the other group had also split up thirty men, well to be precise twenty-nine and one woman were simply too many to move comfortably and cautiously through the passages, rooms and corridors, so fifteen men had split away and set about searching the first floor.

Gustav led his fourteen men up the grand staircase. They carefully opened each door as they came to it along the first landing, empty bedrooms, bathrooms, sitting rooms.

Eight of them would wait either side of the door while the other seven would enter each room, that was in the larger rooms, the bathrooms would only accommodate two or three men at most. Some men had begun to mumble the uselessness of their search as they found room after room empty.

Gustav turned the handle on Anastasia's bedroom door, it was locked. Immediately silence fell like a pall of doom. Gustav pressed his ear to the door, at first it was silent. The men's first reaction was to tighten their grip on their weapons as they watched the expression on Gustav's face change.

"Something is moving about in there." Gustav stepped back from the door, the men gathered around while Gustav prepared to kick the door down. He was not a big man but as with most of the village men he was weathered and hard. At his first assault the door and its surround shuddered. Gustav bounced back falling to the floor. This time he handed his rifle to one of the others. "A little more concentration this time." All eyes were upon him as he made his excuses for failing to demolish the door at his first attempt. Determined to restore his pride he stood back from the door, aimed a kick at the level of the keyhole while one of the others standing to one side held down the handle. Wood splintered and cracked, the door burst open.

Gustav with the impetus of his assault on the door hurtled through the opening, throwing himself flat on the floor, catching only a glimpse of the figure silhouetted against the windows on the far side of the room, his ears rent with the screams that echoed throughout the bedchamber.

Six men poured through the opening, jumping over Gustav's prone body. Out of sheer terror the first man through emptied both barrels of his shotgun toward the figure on the other side of the room. The others followed suit with volley after volley of shots, both rifle and shot gun until there was nothing standing. The windows were shattered stained with splattered blood.

Gustav rose to his feet, someone passed him his shotgun while the others hastily reloaded their weapons. They inched their way around the room standing in a semi-circle around the bloodied heap in the front of the windows.

"Who is it?" the villager's voice was quavering as it spoke.

Gustav replied. "My God, its a woman." But before he could say any more the body shifted, everyone took a step backwards tightening their grips on their weapons.

"Wait" called Gustav.

Val's tattered blood-stained body rolled on the floor, from underneath Anastasia, herself covering in blood, rose unable to speak. Terrified and shaking she just stood surrounded by the villagers with Val's mutilated corpse at her feet. Miraculously Anastasia had not been hit by any shot or bullets.

Nobody said a word, the men stared at Anna and three cautiously glanced at each other. then they heard the clamour of the other group running up the staircase. When they got to the doorway everybody asked at once. "What is it." "Have you got him?" Dan, Stubbs and Eva all realised what had happened at the same time. "Oh! my God, what have you done?" Eva's cry was bitter and scornful.

Dan and Stubbs pushed the villagers out of their way roughly to grumbles of discontent which they totally ignored. Dan took Anna in his arms, asked her if she was hurt. She just shook her head and burst into tears. Dan held her tight then led her through the group of villagers and took her to the room that he had once occupied where they sat on the bed. Dan did his best to comfort her.

Stubbs turned Val's body over. "Jeezus! You bloody stupid murdering bastards." Then he had to repeat himself in French for Eva to translate for the villagers. Gustav blurted out their excuses saying it all happened so quickly and how were they to know she wasn't one of the creatures anyway. There followed a heated argument between Eva and the villagers until Stubbs took Eva by the arm and led her down the landing to the bedroom that Dan and Anna were sitting in.

"We are better off staying here and leave it to them." Stubb's voice had a touch of despair in its tone, not something Dan expected to hear. He had been so determined to get to the Count himself.

"How could I have been so naive?" Anna sobbed. "All these years. My own brother, a monster. He's gone made now. Val and I hid in the passageway last night then this morning made our way toward the stables but Manfred found us and locked us in my room. Then later those men burst in we didn't know what was happening. Oh God!"

Anna burst into tears again unable to finish her tale of the events that day. Dan again comforted her. Eva sat down on the bed next to Anna and put her arm around her. She spoke to Stubbs in French, Stubbs then nodding towards Eva said to Dan.

"Come on, Dan, let's make this room safe for the time being. Dan let Eva take the sobbing Anna from his caress and stood to join Stubbs.

"If he's anywhere in the castle Keith, he will probably be in the catacombs or his lab, he's definitely not up here and there is no fresh scent of him, none more recent than this morning and please don't ask me how I know, that's his doing too."

Eva and Anna stood up. Anna took a deep breath and composed herself. "You are not leaving us here with my mad brother and those gun happy idiot village men roaming about this cursed castle."

Both Stubbs and Dan knew it would be pointless to argue the point and perhaps they were right anyway.

"OK, let's check out the lab and these catacombs." Stubbs asserted, but before he could say any more Dan put in. "The lab OK, but you might as well forget the catacombs. You could easily lose a herd of elephants in that place and he could use any one of dozens of secret exits into the countryside. Besides, if they are locked from the inside it's a pretty safe bet he is not down there."

"Let's go see shall we. But first we must stop in the Great Hall where Manfred keeps all his guns."

Anna seemed to have regained all her confidence. Dan couldn't help thinking "This is one touch woman."

They made their way down the stairs. Dan felt very self-conscious as he sniffed the air of the Great Hall before they entered. "He's not here" was all Dan said. Stubbs smashed the panelling on the cupboard that Anna indicated and took out three twelve gauge shotguns handing one each to Eva, Anna and Dan. He then broke open a drawer containing several boxes of cartridges. Keeping only his .38 revolver for himself he passed out the cartridges to the three of them.

"Well, let's do it. Lead the way, Dan."

More intent on checking the air than brandishing his weapon Dan led the way down towards the lab, instantly picking up the multitude of different smells given off by the research animals. Dan was surprised himself when he realised he could easily differentiate between each one let alone each species, but still no strong recent scent of the Count. They entered each room cautiously even though Dan had said he did not think he was down there.

The doors to the alchemy room and the catacombs were padlocked. "He can't be in there if they are locked from this side." As soon as Dan spoke Anna contradicted him. "He could, Dan. There are secret passages in this place, remember. We know of only one, there are probably more."

They all agreed the futility of searching for secret passages and turned to retrace their steps back up to the ground floor and see what the village men had found, if anything. Half way up the stairs the shooting started. All four broke into a run to the top of the stairs.

"Where is it coming from?" Stubbs blurted out.

"Upstairs, but I couldn't sense the Count's presence up there before." Dan retorted.

"Well, someone can now." Stubbs hissed.

Just then shrieks and yells interrupted by gunshots grew louder as a dozen men came into view at the top of the staircase, fighting and stumbling over each other in their efforts to flee from whatever was up there.

At the same time August and his men came running through the entrance stopping suddenly in the entrance hall staring at the dozen men's panic stricken descent of the staircase. More shrieks and gunshots came from somewhere upstairs, then as suddenly as it had started all fell silent.

The men who had fled from upstairs ignored the questions from their fellow and pushed their way through the crowd out into the courtyard. August grabbed Gustav by his jacket. "What happened?" he bellowed.

"It's up there, it's horrible, it will kill us all. Let me go. Let me go." Gustav spat the last few words out then pulled himself free of August's grasp heading out of the main door.

August seemed the only one of the villagers to be in control. He started giving orders out and went from room to room tearing down curtains and piling furniture on to the staircase though no one wanted to go all the way up.

August then tore some of the cloth from the curtains and wrapped it around the broken leg of a table. He then lit it. When it was burning freely he tossed it into the pile of furniture and curtains on the stairs shouting "Bullets may not get it, but the fire will."

It didn't take long for the blaze to catch and spread up the old wooden staircase catching the tapestries on the walls. The villagers started to push back towards the door as the flames and heat grew.

Then a great gasp rose from the throats of those still in the hall (Stubbs, Dan, Anna and Eva included) as the creature appeared at the head of the stairs, a dripping lump of flesh falling from its jaw as it let out its terrifying howl.

Everyone backed away in fear unable to look away from the thing, the smoke was beginning to sting their eyes. Through the rising smoke and flames they barely saw the creature turn and lope away deeper into the castle. Everyone got out of the door just before the smoke became too thick for them to breath.

The villagers already outside had begun making and lighting fire torches. August then organised them into groups spreading out around the castle throwing the burning torches through every window and open door at ground level. By the time Dan, Anna, Stubbs and Eva had reached the wagons the ground floor of the castle was ablaze and beginning to spread to the upper floors.

When all the villagers regrouped at the carts they checked their numbers. Eighteen men were missing. "There is no help for them now." August declared solemnly.

At that moment they heard the howling again and after a long mournful wail that sent a shiver down the spine of everyone there, the flames engulfed the entire castle spreading to the stables, sending plumes of thick black smoke into the clear afternoon sky. The heat was so intense that everyone moved on down the road climbing into the carts and heading towards the village. The men muttering to each other, mostly reassuring each other that the fire would destroy the beast.

As they wound their way down the hillside the roar of the flames died away. The last thing they heard was a bloodcurdling scream cum howl.

"I think Manfred has gone to his maker." Anna whispered to Dan. Dan replied in an effort to console Anna. "He should be at peace now, Anna."

Nobody spoke again after that until they reached the village where the men set about dismantling the fire traps they had left to protect the women.

That evening there was a meeting in August's tavern. It was decided to say nothing of the werewolf but simply to say the men and servants and the Count were killed in the fire nobody knows how it started.

As the people drifted home there was a bright orange glow on the horizon lighting the night sky with an eerie cast over the landscape.

Chapter 11

RETURN TO ENGLAND

❧

"I T LOOKS LIKE it's over." Keith translated for Dan and Anna. "Is it? I still have the effects of that serum he put into me, what is it going to do to me?" Dan's voice sounded as if he had given up all hope of returning to a normal life.

Anastasia too had a dilemma, with the burning of the castle there was nothing left for her future. All the family assets were kept there, even down to the Count's cash supply. He kept no bank accounts from which Anna could now draw.

"I suppose I will have to find work and somewhere to live." Anna did not sound very enthusiastic about the prospect of it.

Stubbs seemed to be deep in thought before he spoke. "You could both return to England with me, but you'll have to face your charges, Dan."

Dan was stunned. "What do you know of the charges against me?"

He sat open mouthed as Stubbs told them who he really was, explaining that he had come to find out about the Count this time and was not chasing Dan. He also explained that he had come to like and trust Dan and would do everything he could to make things easy for him.

"Do you want to tell me your side of what happened in England, Dan?" Stubbs' tone was at least reassuring and Dan felt after everything he had been through he had nothing to lose, after all British prison couldn't be anywhere near as bad as the dungeons in the castle.

Eva begged them to stay there with her but Stubbs argued that the authorities had to be informed of the Count's demise, even if only for Anna to acquire a new passport and papers, as everything had been destroyed in the fire.

The next day Stubbs, Anna and Dan left for Zyiec, Eva and two of the men from the village accompanied them travelling in a horse drawn cart.

The weather had turned cold and after a few hours travelling Dan had to lay in the back of the cart wrapped in blankets. He was shivering and convulsing violently. Anna sat trying to soothe him, occasionally he would settle into a fitful sleep only to wake up rambling incoherently. Anna kept on saying that they must get him to a hospital only to be answered each time by Stubbs saying "It is probably the Count's serum affecting him, the doctors and hospitals will not be able to do much for him. I think we must let this fever run its course and wait and see how he feels when he comes out of it."

Anna was angry with Stubbs almost screaming at him. "How can you be so complacent, how would you like to be in Dan's shoes right now?"

"Anna" Stubbs' voice was sad and almost hypnotic. "I have been in a similar position a long time ago, not quite the same but near enough, except that I was alone in the forests of Quebec. As you can see, I came through it though it was not pleasant."

Anna was silent for quite some time then she just stared into Stubbs' eyes trying to see what secrets were hidden there but she eventually gave up, returning her attention to the now sleeping Dan.

By late evening the group had taken three rooms in an old inn on the edge of Zyiec. The innkeeper had not been too keen to let Dan stay but between Eva and Anna they managed to persuade him saying he just had a touch of influenza.

The two ladies put Dan to bed leaving the two villagers and Stubbs to order their supper. Eva joined them a few minutes later saying that Anna did not want to eat, she would rather sit with Dan to comfort him. The four ate their meal in silence and soon retired for the night.

Eva was quiet and unable to read Keith's mood. She did not want this to be their last night together although try as she might she had not been able to make Stubbs change his mind over returning to England.

Dan woke next morning feeling a little shaky but a lot better. All Anna could get out of him was how hungry he was for a rare steak. When they met the others at breakfast he settled for bacon, bread and hot coffee.

Eva looked as if she had been crying and Stubbs hardly spoke a word over their food. Anna wanted to ask Eva if she were alright but thought better of it after the furtive glances she kept giving Stubbs.

Breakfast was just about finished as five policemen walked into the room. One of the policemen spoke to them, despite Dan and Stubbs not understanding them.

"You are all from the village near Versipellis castle, yes?" They were all taken aback when Anna was the first to speak up.

"Yes, we have come from the village, I am Anastasia Versipellis, what is this all about?"

"My Lady, I must ask you and your companions to accompany us to the police station. In the early hours of this morning we received news of a grave nature. I cannot say more at the moment, when we get to the station one of my superiors will explain things to you."

Anna turned to Stubbs and explained what the policemen had said. Stubbs advised her that for now it was best to go along with them but added. "Don't volunteer too much information about your brother's demise until we know what had happened."

Everybody was then bundled into three police cars and taken to the local station. The landlord complained bitterly that nobody had been given a change to pay their bill.

⤝✦⤞

Not a single cottage was left intact, mutilated corpses lay everywhere. The young policeman who had journeyed to the village in the early hours was a nephew of August. It was pure coincidence he had travelled overnight from Warsaw to visit his uncle.

On arriving at the devastated village he had been shocked and violently sick before turning tail and driving hell for leather into Zyiec to report his findings to the local police. How the local police had found out about Anna and her party nobody said.

When they were informed of the happenings at the village all six were shocked, their fears that the Count had not perished in the fire at the castle surging to the forefront of their thoughts. Then the realisation struck them, who in this day and age in modern society would believe in werewolves. It was more likely that they were the only candidates on which to lay the blame for the slaughter and burning of the village.

Stubbs switched himself into his official police inspector mode and insisted that they were taken to Kracow Police Headquarters. This happened only after two days in the cells and the local Chief of Police was satisfied that Stubbs actually was who he claimed to be.

The following day all six were transported to Kracow. On arrival at Headquarters Stubbs once again met up with

Niko who had been allocated to him and Dan as interpreter. He hadn't recognised him straight away but as soon as Stubbs spoke to him recognition washed over his face. Dan had started drifting in and out of his fever again and was taken under guard to hospital, the police had given up on any thoughts of trying to interrogate him.

They eventually settled on Stubbs' statement and accepted that to travel from the village to Zyiec by horse and cart they must have left well before the village was destroyed. Niko explained to Stubbs that they had put down most of the killings to robbers and bandits though who, nobody had any idea.

The only tracks leaving the desolated village were those of animals which in part at least must have been responsible for the demise of most of the people as they all seemed partly eaten to some degree but nobody would say whether they had been eaten before or after their deaths.

The hospital put Dan's condition down to anaemia and he seemed greatly improved after a transfusion of several pints of blood, after which he as released into police custody until a flight home for he and Stubbs was arranged.

The authorities would not let Anastasia leave the country until an investigation into the events at the castle and its burning down, also the disappearance of her brother was thoroughly looked into. This was, of course, despite the fact that all concerned had already decided that the outcome of such an investigation would prove as effective as had the investigation into the demise of the villagers and their homes.

Still, Anastasia was the last in a long line of nobility and would be treated with just accord. The two villagers had simply disappeared on their release from police headquarters. Anna insisted that Eva stay with her, at least until they both found some direction in which to turn.

Dan's and Anna's also Stubbs' and Eva's goodbyes were to say the least awkward in the uninvited police presence at the airport. Dan and Stubbs turned and walked away looking back to wave only once after their embarrassment of public caresses. Both men feeling that the police might have given them at least a little privacy. Both women had tears in their eyes. Anna especially wondered what would happen to Dan and if they would ever see each other again.

On the flight home Dan talked his heart out to Stubbs telling him everything in the hope that he might have some influence with his colleagues in England. Stubbs didn't say much, he simply listened and when Dan had finished his only comment was "Well, I think you have already been punished enough, but that is not for me to decide, we will have to see what the Courts think about it. Best to leave out the werewolf side of your story though, you don't want to end up in the nut house, do you? The London School has records of the Count's immoral and illegal activities and his premature departure under a cloud of suspicion. If we can get hold of those records it should help your case considerably."

Harris and two constables were waiting at Heathrow to meet Stubbs and Dan. Harris' first remarks to Stubbs were straight to the point.

"Are you in for some trouble matey. What the hell have you been up to?"

Stubbs just looked Harris in the eye and said nothing, he simply turned to Dan and said quietly "Well, let's face the music, eh."

Nobody was more surprised that Dan when the two thugs who had attempted to mug him turned up in court as witness for his defence. When they admitted that the three of them had attempted to brutally rob him that evening and with the testimony Keith Stubbs provided in praise of Dan's character the Judge to the Courts acquitted Dan of the charge of wilful manslaughter, but he did give Dan a twelve month suspended sentence for absconding from justice.

Rather than face the severe disciplinary action after the court case Stubbs decided to tender his resignation to the police force.

He and Dan left the court and all the memories it had stirred up behind them and set about finding somewhere quiet.

They talked frequently of sending for Anna and Eva but in the six months it had taken to settle the trial they had both only ever received a single letter from the ladies.

It was only now that they realised just how time consuming the trial had been. Stubbs especially so as he had spent a lot of time subtly persuading the two thugs to testify on Dan's behalf.

Chapter 12

SOUNDS OF THE CITY

❧❦❧

D AN WOKE EVERY morning listening to the sounds around him, neighbours' conversations, unseen insects scurrying in cupboards. He would sniff the air and arouse his senses, here just as keen as ever, thinking to himself. I must remember to put on my sunglasses before I draw the blinds today. He did not always remember to his extreme discomfort when the morning light seared his sensitive eyes. He always wore them in any level of daylight.

When Stubbs had quit the force he had been offered a position with a firm of private detectives just outside London in Surrey and having been given free rein to pick his cases he took Dan along as his assistant.

Stubbs being the only person aware of Dan's abilities, his colleagues being stunned at the speed and success of the cases they handled. Mostly diverse work, but detecting whether a woman has been with a man other than her husband or vice versa was no more than a couple of seconds of a chance meeting by way of work for Dan. Once they knew picking up evidence was fairly easy for Stubbs.

Keith and Dan shared a fairly spacious house that Stubbs had bought after selling his place in town. It had used up most of his savings but it was big enough for the two men not to be in each others way all the time. Besides after two years they had more money than they needed to keep a more than adequate home between them.

Stubbs did not worry when Dan would disappear off into the country some week-ends. His excuse being that the town and city's noise and pollution would get too much for him.

Dan's favourite retreat was generally the New Forest. He would either camp out in his car or stay at one of the many bed and breakfast hotels in the area, although he used these establishments infrequently.

Preferring to wander into the deeper more secluded areas of woodland such as Pennywood he would always cross fences and boundaries. He could never resist a stroll through Stubbswood out near Beaulieu Road and wander or just sit for hours, even days, his acute senses picking up every movement in the woods. How much ordinary people missed he often thought which always led him into thinking of how he came about his present condition.

As he returned to the city he was nauseated by the sounds and smells growing more pungent every day adding to his fine sensitivities, adding more to his feelings of despondency.

He simply buried himself in the detective work he and Stubbs had undertaken. At least he felt he was a little special and his talents in that field were at least appreciated if not fully understood by anyone other than Keith Stubbs.

Chapter 13

SPECIAL CLIENT

❧❧❧

T HE PHONE RANG at about 11.30am Monday morning.
 "Hello, Keith Stubbs here."

"Good morning Keith, it's Stan, I'm boss of the company you work for, if you remember."

"OK, Stan, enough sarcasm. I presume you have a job for us."

Stan Tyler had his own way of dealing with the lack of control he had over Stubbs and Dan, but he was sensible enough to realise how valuable they were to him.

"Keith, I've had an enquiry from a Mr Matthew Farnham from a place called Tarporley in Cheshire. He's got a daughter gone missing but doesn't want to involve the police. He asked for you and Dan specifically, but don't ask me how he heard about you. I don't have a clue. To be honest he took me so by surprise I forgot to ask. Though he did happen to mention that money would be no object so I assured him that in all probability you would accept the case."

"OK, Stan, Dan and I will come into the office this afternoon and discuss it with you. See you later, bye."

The Cheshire police had confirmed several reports of missing girls all within the last six month's period. Stan Tyler had asked them for any information which may help with a case his firm were looking into. They were sceptical at first but Tyler could be very persuasive and did have some very influencial connections. As soon as he received the faxed copies of six missing girl reports, after briefly glancing through them, he left them in Stubbs' and Dan's in-tray.

What did puzzle him was why the Cheshire police had received no contact from the mysterious Mr Farnham. Farnham had told Tyler that he was something of a recluse owing to a disfiguring accident some years ago and did not enjoy the kind of publicity that came with a police investigation such as this.

It was mid-afternoon when Stubbs and Dan finally arrived at the office. After looking over the files and Mr Farnham's report on his daughter's disappearance Stubbs argued with Tyler over taking it on, saying that it wasn't really the kind of thing they handled. Tyler argued that he didn't have anyone better and they had been specifically asked for anyway.

"Come on, Keith, it wouldn't hurt just to go up there and talk to the man, would it?" Tyler pleaded with him. "Besides he is offering a substantial figure even for just a consultation."

"How did this guy know of us anyway, Stan?" It was a question that had stuck in the back of Stubbs' mind and it seemed to bother the usually unflappable Canadian.

"No idea Keith, he didn't say, well, will you go?"

"OK we will drive up in the morning, and we will need some expenses, two hundred pounds should cover it. Happy now Stan?"

As usual when money was mentioned Tyler started puffing and blowing and whining like an old woman, but eventually parted with £200 of his beloved cash.

Stubbs drove his Ford Granada steadily north up the M6. It was a miserable, dull wet day. Dan complained almost all the way.

"Why did we let Farnham talk us into this, it's not as if we're desperate for work?"

Stubbs didn't answer he knew it was best simply to leave Dan to his complaining when he was in these moods.

They stopped for a bite to eat and some coffee at the motorway services before their turnoff. After eating they freshened up and then set off on the last leg of their journey.

Finding their way to the village of Tarporley they pulled up outside a large set of wrought iron gates. Dan was just about to get out of the car to see if there was a bell on the gates when the automatically swung open. Closing his door Dan sat and watched as Stubbs drove up the gravel driveway, twisting and turning through trees and bushes as the gates behind them closed, clanging noisily as they disappeared from sight.

Round the next turn the house came into sight, large square fronted but not as big as they had expected for such a gravel driveway. Tyres crunching on the gravel Stubbs pulled up outside the front door.

"I don't like this place, let's just turn around and go." Stubbs could sense an urgency in Dan's request and also noticed the glint of fear in his eyes. Something he hadn't really ever expected to see again.

"What is it Dan, can you sense or see something?"

"I don't know for sure Keith, it's just," Dan paused in thought for a moment "just a little paranoia, I suppose. I'm feeling a bit on edge at the moment, and I don't know why."

Without further comment the two men got out of the car and started up the stone steps that led to the front door. Before they had a chance to knock a tall heavy man in a blue suit opened the door, stepping aside so the pair could walk straight in at his invitation, be it only a gesture. The man did not speak at all. The door slammed shut behind them and three men, all dressed in similar fashion stepped into the hallway and to their sudden shock Dan and Stubbs noticed two of them held revolvers, pointed at them.

On of the men with a gun instructed the two unarmed men to search Dan and Stubbs. Once this was done, having found no weapons on either of the two men they were ushered into another room. As they were guided into what was furnished as a sitting room, Dan quietly whispered to Stubbs.

"He's here. I wasn't sure at first but the bastard is not dead."

Before Stubbs could question Dan's statement they were pushed down to sit on a large settee. At the same moment a hideously scarred man walked into the room from another door, but despite his disfigurement Stubbs instantly recognised his host, mostly from his stature and a head of long grey hair than from that burnt face. He was too stunned to speak and Dan immediately sensed the instant wave of fear washing through his partner as they both stared at a man, or thing, they had believed to be dead.

In front of them stood Count Manfred Versippelis.

"You two have made a very good job of turning my life upside down. I have still not decided on an appropriate course of action in respect of my revenge. But now you are my guests I'm sure I will come up with something appropriate."

Without giving them a chance to speak the Count turned and left the room by the door he had entered. Dan and Stubbs were then taken to a room on the first floor that looked like it had been completely encased in steel plate including door and ceiling. In the room were two cot type beds with mattresses but nothing else. The door was closed and locked behind them.

They both simply sat on the boards in silence not wanting to believe their situation. Both too stunned to speak, they sat for what seemed hours, both staring into space.

After what seemed forever to Dan and Stubbs the door opened and the two men with their guns appeared, they ushered both men back downstairs and into another room. The sight of this room totally unnerved Dan sending waves of fear through him. The room was plainly set up as a surgery with two operating tables in the centre of the room.

They were taken then through a door on the other side of the room. In total contract to the surgery this was a plush sitting room in which the Count was sitting waiting for them. They were told to sit on a couch facing the armchair occupied by the Count.

In the dim light of the room it was difficult to make out the full extent of the Count's disfigurement. Once seated the two bodyguards moved into the shadows of the couch and stood silently.

"I suppose you are intrigued as to how I escaped the fiery end your planned for me. I think I can tell you how and also a little more besides.

The Count then in his low whispery voice proceeded to relate his tale to Dan and Stubbs.

"With the flames all about me in the form of my own hair and flesh burning drove me deep into the west wing of the castle. My eyes were stinging from the smoke but I could just see enough to detect that a stream of air was pulling the smoke into an interior room, then disappearing through a crack between the bookshelves. I had always been aware that there were many passageways and tunnels throughout the castle, some I myself did not even know about."

"I made the fastest transformation I had ever done and groped in the heat and smoke for the trigger, finding it only just before I was about to pass out from the smoke choking me. I gulped fresh air whilst crawling on my hands and knees when the panel in the bookshelf burst open. Recovering my wits I once again turned myself into my other state as I could make much better progress on four legs rather than two.

The passage eventually led me to the catacombs with which, as you know, I am very familiar. From there it was simple to make my way to the woods and as I am sure you would guess survival in the wild is well within my capabilities. I spent longer than I ever had as the creature. This in itself made survival easier and it also speeded up the recovery of my wounds which at that time were quite severe. Though I am improving as time goes on and eventually you would not know anything have even happened to me, one of the pluses of my condition."

Their little lecture went on for some hours as he told of how he let six months go by then turned up in Krakov and collected a safety deposit box with a substantial amount of cash and other personal papers put away in an alias and then proceeded to build up his position again. Slipping out of Poland and into West Europe eventually settling in Cheshire, England intending to bide his time here until he could make a full recovery from his burns.

"I have been in this house for about nine months now." The Count seemed proud of his achievements, but showed very little bitterness towards Dan and Stubbs.

"And now to another well-kept secret my friends, you see all I told you about my ancestry but I left out several facts. For, one, I am a little over two hundred years old, two, your sweet Anastasia whom I warned you stay away from is actually my daughter, although she doesn't know it. Now the thing is although I have lived a long time my family think she is the only one capable of definitely continuing the blooding."

Shocked Dan spoke up. "You actually intend to produce another of these creatures that you are by raping your own daughter. Damn, you're sick."

"Your opinions Dan do not interest me, what does interest me is your success in detective work. you, Mr Stubbs, are an efficient detective and with Dan's, shall we say abilities for which I take full responsibility, you have both done very well. The task I want of you Mr Stubbs, is exactly what I contacted your firm for. You see while I keep Dan here for security I want you to find and bring back Anastasia."

He paused giving Stubbs time to think over his proposition. "Well, Mr Stubbs, I believe you have seen the alternatives." Another pause while he studied Stubb's face as he tried to work out what the Count meant.

"Surely you did pass through the operating room. A person with your background should prove a very interesting study."

"Alright Count, I'll go to find Anastasia but I will make you another promise." This time it was Stubb's turn to study the puzzlement on the Count's face, finally adding

"A promise I will keep one day, I will return and kill you."

The vacancy of emotion in Stubbs' tone made the statement twice as effective though the Count showed no sign of being intimidated by it. He simply chose to ignore it. Giving orders to Johnson and Patrick to accompany Mr Stubbs first to London and then to Poland to find Anastasia.

Stubbs and Dan were then returned to their room while preparations for the trip to Poland were made.

The Count made sure that Johnson and Patrick understood their mission and were to kill Stubbs if anything were to go wrong or once they had found Anastasia and she was in their company. He stressed she was not to be harmed but Stubbs must die one way or the other.

Later that night Dan's and Stubbs' prison door opened and Stubbs was escorted out leaving Dan alone with Keith Stubbs' words still running around in his head.

"Don't hesitate to escape if you can Dan, one I am away I should be able to take care of these two bozos, but I have no idea how long it might take. So let yourself out of here the first opportunity, OK."

Dan had agreed, he did not need persuading that the less time he spent in the Count's company the better.

Chapter 14

SECOND ESCAPE

❦

FOR TWO DAYS the Count had Dan brought to his study and spent most of the afternoon bragging to Dan of his many killings, especially his most recent in the surrounding area. He gloated over the fact that local police were totally baffled and people around were getting more and more reluctant to venture out after dark.

One or two motorists had reported glimpsing a huge wolf-like dog running through Delamere Forest, a local beauty spot for picnickers and ramblers. But the police in their naivety didn't for one second think of connecting it to the killings. They were convinced this was the work of another Jack the Ripper character and put all their efforts into tracking down all known criminally insane previous offenders almost country-wide.

It was on this afternoon that Dan noticed that the snap of the lock as it opened for him to be taken to the Count was not as sharp a sound as it had usually been, with this on his mind he was even more aware of its sound as he returned to his cell.

What should have been a sharp click was definitely much deeper than before. At first he thought it was just age and wear and tear. But the more he thought about it the more he thought the Count had this room constructed especially for him, supposedly escape proof, so the lock should be brand new.

He still had a silver ballpoint pen in his jacket pocket. Removing the outer case the refill cartridge was made of thin aluminium, not very strong, Dan thought, but what the hell, to give it a try was better than nothing.

He slipped the point of the cartridge into the gap where the deadlock was and tried to lever it back and with a little effort just before the cartridge looked about to snap the lock gave. It sounded like a cannon going off to Dan. He waited holding his breath listening intently. All he could hear were muffled sounds from downstairs.

The daylight was beginning to fade, it had been a dark cloudy overcast day anyway and the upstairs corridor was shadowed and still. As Dan eased the door fully open his pulse beginning to quicken as the adrenalin coursed through him.

He turned closing the door and moved silently away from the staircase leading down to where the Count and his two thugs sat. He could hear their voices quite audibly now although far too distant for any normal persons ears to pick up. The conversation was on the lines of both men getting well paid for some presumably grisly task the Count wished them too perform.

Dan eased open a door at the end of the hallway, his keen eyes picking out each detail in the rapidly diminishing light. It looked as it if was the bedroom of one of the bodyguards, he crossed carefully wary of any creaky floorboards eventually reaching the window on the opposite wall.

The catch was stiff but with a sharp tug it snapped open. Again, to Dan it sounded like a rifle shot as he once more held his breath and listened, he was sweating freely even though the air was chilled.

The next step seemed to Dan to go on forever, the rumble as he lifted the sash window open, surely they would hear that.

"No time to find out, get out of here." Dan wasn't sure whether he had whispered that to himself or just thought it.

"What was that?" the Count paused listening intently.

"Go and take a look it came from upstairs, and check Hunter's room.

Both Steadman and Brookes, the Count's two bodyguards, although more like overgrown errand boys, raced up the stairs on the Count's command. Neither of the men were bright enough to contemplate the hold Manfred Versippelis had over them, but he paid well so they never complained regardless of how weird their tasks became.

As they reached the top of the stairs they saw Dan's cell door hanging open. Brookes turned and started down the stairs stopping half way he yelled at the top of his voice.

"He's out Sir, doors open, I don't know how, the door was defin . . . ." The Count cut him off in mid sentence, his temper flaring so fast Brookes almost shook.

"Find him now, he must not get away."

Brookes turned and started up the stairs but was stunned when the Count passed him before he reached the top. Steadman had just checked the room which converted to a cell for Dan.

Dan's ears picked up Brookes and Steadman's footfalls as they climbed the stairs and realising the time for caution had gone he let himself dangle from the window ledge at arm's length then dropped into the dark below hopeful there were no obstacles on the way down.

His feet hit the gravel path, letting his knees buckle he collapsed with a loud crunch and gasped as the landing knocked the breath from his body. Breathing deeply he staggered to his feet expecting either to give way having broken something; his thighs, knees and ankles throbbed from the impact but none were damaged and as soon as he realised it he was up and running across the lawn.

It seemed to Dan only seconds after he started to run when he heard someone shouting "He's out."

That was enough to spur Dan to greater speed. It was only moments later, he seemed miles from the bushes that would at least give him some cover when he heard the second shout.

"This way, he's got out of Eddie's window." There his across the lawn."

Dan clearly heard that, thinking while he was running, Eddie must be one of the Count's lackeys.

He was getting closer to the bushes and trees now, but his heart gave a leap as he hear the shots ring out. He felt the fourth shot whistle past his ear as he dove head long into the bushes, ignoring the cuts and scratching as branches and brambles tore at him.

He scrambled dog-like on all fours through the dense parts of shrubbery thinking how ironic that was being as it was the very fate he was trying to escape.

Dan's eyes easily taking in enough light to see clearly even in the most dense sections of undergrowth this was the only advantage he had. He could now make out the brickwork of the perimeter wall as he scrambled through the last few yards of the Count's property.

It was at this moment he lost his advantage, floodlights came on all over the grounds. Dan's heart sunk (if it could sink much more) but he would die before he would give up.

Coming to his feet he took a flying leap at the six foot wall and managed to grab hold of the top of the wall, his feet scrambled against the crumbling mossy brickwork but inch by inch he gained purchase on the top of the wall. Once his chest was level with the top he was able to pull his weight up and roll first one leg over then the other, dropping in an exhausted heap onto the grass verge once more in the shadow.

He lay motionless for as long as he dare trying to recover his senses. He had put so much effort into getting across the grounds, then over the wall, for a time he felt if he tried to stand he would collapse in a dead faint.

He breathing was returning to a steadier rate when he heard the bushes on the other side of the wall stir from movement within.

It was then he saw the headlights of a car approaching from down the road. Climbing to his feet he made his way towards the oncoming vehicle keeping to the grass so no one could hear his footsteps on the tarmac of the road being unsure of just how acute the Count's hearing was.

As the car closed Dan stepped into the road waving his arms violently in an effort to get the drive to stop.

Jenny Coffee spotted the madman, jumping up and down waving his arms in the road, just in time to swerve to the other lane to avoid him. As she passed him her foot came off the accelerator pedal just long enough to consider whether it was someone in trouble, then the thoughts of recent killings came to the forefront of her mind, she instantly hit the gas and carried on down the road on her way to meet her boyfriend, already planning how she would tell him the story of the madman in the road she was sensible enough to avoid.

Dan didn't have time to feel deserted as the car disappeared in the distance. He started to run down the road in the direction from which the vehicle had come. then his ears picked up on the grating creaking noise of the Count's gate opening some distance behind him and the roar of the car engine being revved in anticipation of getting onto the road. Something about the car sounded wrong then he realised it wasn't one, but two.

To his left was still the wall, Dan didn't know whether it was still the Count's house or not so no escape there. On his right was a hawthorn hedgerow and fields, accelerating he dove over the hedge and landed in a muddy field, totally exhausted.

Steadman, after firing four shots at Dan, collapsed sideways when the Count struck him, and seriously considered emptying the other two bullets from his revolver into the Count, but something in the Count's icy stare told him it would do no good.

"I don't want him dead, you idiot."

The Count had then sent him down to throw on the floodlights and despatched Brookes to the garage to get out the two Mercedes 190s to take Steadman with him and check either way along the road with strict instructions to only wound him and bring him back alive.

In his haste to escape Dan had not realised that the rustling on the other side of the wall was not Steadman or Brookes but a huge silver coloured creature resembling a wolf, but half as big again and missing large clumps of fur here and there. Hearing the approach of the car the creature hesitated at crossing the perimeter wall.

Once the car was out of earshot it cleared the wall with a single bound landing silently just in time to pick out a figure disappearing over the hedgerow a hundred or so metres down the road. Although he stood stationary as the two Mercedes pulled out of the driveway and noticed the expression on the driver's face as one of the cars passed by searching for Dan.

Steadman buzzed Brookes on his walkie-talkie. "Jesus, you wanna see the size of this dog out here, its probably eaten that soft get tryin to escape from the boss."

Brookes' reply was curt. "Keep yer mind on the job, ya know we're gonna get the blame for this, let's just get that bastard back."

Dan was breathing heavily lying behind the hedgerow as the car cruised passed. Suddenly his nostrils flared followed by his stomach heaving, wanting almost to vomit with pure fear. He could smell the creature nearby.

He started to move away when he heard the rustle not more than a hundred metres away. Turning, his keen eyes picked out the silhouette of a huge wolf-like creature softly landing in the field. The same field as he was in now.

Without hesitation Dan launched himself back over the hedge, once in his life would have been enough to face that thing but he had no taste for a second confrontation, especially this time he was alone and defenceless.

Terrified he turned to run down the road but he couldn't be sure as his fear was mixing up his senses but he was sure the creature was shadowing him just on the other side of the hedge. He started bumbling to himself as he ran, his bumbling getting ragged, his mind raced with memories of seeing the huge animal close up. He felt as if the sweat running down his face and neck was the drooling saliva of the creature.

Any second now, Dan thought over and over again waiting for the thing to clear the hedge and have him. It was almost like it was enjoying the chase making him suffer.

Then Dan spotted the headlights of a car coming towards him and prayed that this time it may just stop to help him.

Frantically Dan tried to wave down the approaching car. He had stopped running beginning to believe it futile anyway with that thing shadowing him so easily. What Dan did not realise was that after his escape from the house and his landing in the field, he was covered in mud and in the dim light of the roadway he was almost perfectly camouflaged.

The two young men in the Vauxhall Astra had been drinking quite heavily and their senses and reactions were not at their best although the driver did manage to spot Dan at the last minute and swerved to avoid what seemed to him to be a scarecrow suddenly materialising in the middle of the road.

Unfortunately he didn't miss the thing completely clipping it with the left hand side of the car bonnet sending it high into the air followed by a dull thud as some part of its body bounced off the windscreen spinning it into a bloody heap in the middle of the road.

Skidding the car to a stop both men got out and ran back. All they could make out in the dim light was the crumpled body of what now looked more like a tramp to them.

"He looks dead."

"Then lets get the hell out of here before anybody else comes."

At that the two young men ran back to their car and took off in a hurry. Neither of them noticed the creature watching from the side of the road a few yards up.

As soon as the Count re-entered his house he once again controlled his turning becoming human in form once more. He quickly dressed then called Steadman and Brookes on the walkie-talkies telling them where they would find Dan.

Ten minutes later between them they carried the broken bloodied body into the Count's surgery.

Chapter 15

RECOVERY

❧❖❧

BROOKES HAD PASSED out early on after Dan's clothes had been removed revealing the damage to his body.

He was cut and bruised practically all over but the worst damage was to his left thigh. It was completely snapped and jutted out from the ragged lumps of torn muscle.

Dan's breathing was very shallow but the Count soon had him anaesthetised and his breathing seemed to strengthen becoming more steady.

Steadman assisted the Count as best he could in his own ham-fisted way, although he had to fight to keep his dinner inside his stomach several times, especially when the Count cut through long strips of muscle to release both halves of Dan's snapped thigh bone.

Over the next few hours the Count managed to bind Dan's thigh bone together and then stitch the muscle back in place. It was not a pretty job but the Count was confident of a successful recovery.

That completed the Count sent Steadman for two one litre bottles of blood kept in the refrigerator in the surgery and connected Dan to one to be followed by the other thus completing Dan's transfusion.

The only time Steadman said anything to the Count was to ask whether he knew if the blood would match up to Dan's. He freely accepted the Count's answer despite the fact he did not understand it. He simply thought life was easier the less questions you asked.

As for the Count's response. "But of course it will match up, it's mine."

It was a couple of days later before Dan was properly coherent again. He woke to find the Count sitting on a chair watching him in silence. He was in a normal bedroom this time (still he presumed in the same house).

"Good morning, Daniel, it's nice to have you back with us."

Dan tried to sit up but winced from the pain that shot through his thigh. He then became aware of the heavy strapping to his left leg.

"What happened, I don't remember much."

The Count sat staring at Dan, rubbing his chin with his thumb nail. There was something about him, Dan couldn't quite work out what. then it came to him he was much less scared than he had previously been and then remembered what the Count had told him about how he would recover from his burns in time.

The Count told Dan of the events of his attempted escape and although Dan expected a warning as to further attempts he got none.

After a week in bed Dan was getting restless and when the Count came to visit him he asked if he may get up and try to move about. The Count instantly forbade this saying that the break in his leg was severe and at least another week of rest was necessary, then added although you should heal a lot faster than you may expect.

"And why is that?" Dan asked although he was not sure he would like the answer knowing some of the things the Count was known to do.

"Because, Dan, you can now class yourself as one of the bloodline of the Versipellis, a Turnskin."

Dan's eyes were wide with shock although he could not speak even if he had tried.

"Yes, Dan, the transfusion I gave you was from a store of my own blood which I had prepared over some time for just this sort of eventuality. Now I will leave you to take in what may become of you. Get some rest." With that statement echoing around Dan's mind the Count turned and left the room.

Now Dan felt the total weight of hopelessness about him. The first thing to his mind was suicide but he didn't know if he could.

Later he drifted off to sleep in complete despair. The dreams came. Frightening and real. Running alone, surviving, the taste of warm blood, then running with a pack of wolves, hot steaming fetid breath all around him, then he woke. Sweating, almost panting, shaking with fear. Once more despair.

Again, as every morning, the Count visited Dan, his conversation turning more to lectures of the Count's ancestry. The Count seemed to enjoy watching Dan's fears grow.

"In time you must learn to embrace it as a gift. Do not shy away from it like a curse. Although it will take you a long time to learn to control the beast."

The Count's words weighted heavy on Dan's mind. The Count sensed this and it only seemed to encourage him into talking more of what Dan may expect.

Another of the Count's morning speeches found him telling Dan more of his roots.

"My ancestors didn't just discover one form of werewolf manifestation but several. One form carries immortality, this though is very rare. Another is to be infected by a ingle bite from a living werewolf whilst in its animal state. The other and the most common form is passed down by heredity."

This conversation did manage to distract Dan from his depression spurring him into asking a question of the Count for the first time in ages.

"And to which category do you belong, Count."

"Unfortunately, Dan, I, and presently yourself, fall into the common category although if your transfusion is completely successful you can expect to live at least twice as long as a normal human being, but be careful, while you will heal amazingly quickly you are not immortal.

Again Dan was left for the rest of the day and night with only occasional meal and bed pan visits from Steadman and Brookes.

Another day, another visit, another lecture. This one went along the lines of the folklore truths and half truths behind what people used to believe, not just of werewolves, but other tales which originated from actual conditions, from Norse folklore legends of berserkers and to the Yeti in the Himalayas. Nobody today wants to believe in them. Life is too busy and people prefer to believe in the scientific rather than the supernatural and if anything too outrageous is suspected it is simply ignored so arrogant has man become in his own importance."

"So do you think you could take me into a British Court and have me tried for being a werewolf? You would be committed to an asylum for the rest of your days."

Dan hated all that the Count told him. Mostly because now he had to believe it to be true. But also the burden of keeping it to yourself so as not to be thought of as a lunatic.

Chapter 16

RELEASE

꒦꒷꒦

D AN COULD NOT take in fully the consequence of all that
had now become his lot His leg had healed so quickly hefelt
he could almost see the change from day to day. Two weeks had passed
since his ordeal of attempted escape and the medical care the Count
had given him.

Over and over in his mind turned the weight of the Count's
statement after he had received all that blood.

Was it true? He was nauseous with worry and had hardly slept
since. In fact he tried his damndest not to sleep in fear of what might
happen.

The odd times he did drift away he was permanently beset by
nightmares, some of which were similar to those he used to have
before all this happened. Running through woodland hotly pursued,
falling, but this time he effected his escape with comparative ease. He
would often wake feeling exhausted in the satisfaction of evading his
tormentors, sweating and breathing heavily.

Each morning the Count would visit his room and each visit he
would comment on Dan's condition, then gloat.

"Another bad dream, no need to worry yet! There is time before
your dreams merge with reality. But don't fret I will release you to

your own freedom, if you can call it that, before you are in any real danger of turning . . .''

The next few days passed with only occasional visits from the Count.

Dan's burden was growing with the effort of trying to stay awak 24 hours a day. Time once again, as it had in the dungeons of the castle, had become immaterial.

Dan woke from fitful slumber and immediately sensed something different. He gingerly stepped from his bed testing his bad leg. Being not as surprised as he had expected to be when he found it fully healed. He then walked over to the bedroom door rather unsteady from his weeks of inactivity more than pain of his injury.

The door was open, poking his head out into the hallway he sniffed the air but could not detect the presence of anybody about. He turned back into the room and opening the small wardrobe found his clothes all hanging there. He was in something of a quandry as to why this should be. Surely the Count had greater plans of revenge than simply to allow him to leave an empty house.

After dressing he checked the house but everything had gone. The basic furniture remained but all evidence of the Count and his bodyguards ever having been there had been effectively removed. Efficiently removed because Dan's acute hearing had told him nothing of the goings on in the house. But then he had to accept that the Count was no amateur and knew totally of Dan's abilities and probably his failings too.

Thinking over the Count's comments of the last few weeks Dan came to the conclusion that this is what the Count had intended all along. Not knowing whether he woudl turn completely into a werewolf and what would happen if he did was a greater punishment than was ever deserved for any crime. nothing to look forward to but a life of fear and uncertainty.

To hell with the future Dan decided. "Lets get out of here while the getting is good."

The gates were open as Dan shakily made his way down the gravel pathway out onto the road. To his utter amazement his wallet was still in his jacket pocket along with his sunglasses which he put on, although it was a cloudy overcast day.

He trundled down the road passing other grand gate and driveways eventually coming upon a phone box. He called Stan Tyler.

Chapter 17

DETECTIVE'S DILEMMA

❧❀❧

STUBBS KNEW HE could not trust the Count to keep his word and release them once he had returned Anastasia to him. He also thought of Anna's feeling if she was forced into the plans her brother, or was it her father, intended for her.

The Count's two thugs, Johnson and Dobbs travelled to Surrey with Stubbs and made themselves at home in his and Dan's house.

Johnson had the list of outgoing flights to Poland which the Count had given him then told Stubbs to get his passport and called British Airways to book the flight to Krakow.

The drawer Stubbs rummaged through was not the one in which he kept his passport but it did have his revolver in it.

Dobbs was standing right behind Stubbs so as Stubbs' hand closed over the grip of the revolver he turned quickly pushing the barrel into Dobbs' throat whilst taking a firm hold on his jacket so as not to let him pull away.

"OK! then chaps. First Johnson take out your gun and put it on the floor."

Johnson reached into his jacket slowly. It then became apparent that he had no concern over the fate of his partner. The 9 millimetre automatic was pointing straight at Stubbs. Johnson's voice was cold and calm.

"Catch 22, Mr Stubbs. Drop the weapon."

Stubbs knew he would not get another chance after this and if he did drop the gun he was probably in line for a good kicking from either, or both men. He could feel his pulse speed up and the adrenalin started to course through him as he thought. "Go for it, now, don't hesitate."

He roughly pushed Dobbs as hard as he could towards Johnson and started to drop down onto one knee, but Johnson was a little quicker than he had anticipated. Two rounds from his automatic shattered the silence followed by the anguished gurgling cry from Dobbs as one of Johnson's bullets passed through his back and lodged in his lung. The second bullet, closer to its mark, ripped through Stubbs' shoulder making him lurch back into the desk he now kneeled in front of.

Without any hesitation, even before he regained his balance, Stubbs fired back emptying three .38 bullets into Johnson's chest with unerring accuracy. There was just one more shot fired, it came from Johnson's gun as he hand clenched in spasm before he died. Stubbs fell to the floor as he felt the last bullet burning way deep into his chest, then felt a hopelessness as everything drifted into a murky black pool, then nothing.

After finding the three bodies at Stubbs' and Dan's house the police were satisfied that it was just these three who were involved.

They contacted Stan Tyler but the only information he could give them was that since their last assignment he had heard nothing from them for several days.

The police paid Matthew Farnham a visit in Tarporley whereupon the old grey haired crippled man told them Stubbs and Hunter had refused his request to look for his daughter and left within hours of their visit which was some days ago now. He gave the police no reason to suspect him. The only thing puzzling them was Dan's disappearance.

Johnson and Dobbs were known to the police as bully boys involved in protection, extortion and a multitude of other petty crimes. This time it seemed an estranged lover or spouse had hired them to take revenge on Stubbs and possibly Dan for exposing them one way or another. That meant looking through all their case files.

He awoke shivering, lying naked on a cold stainless steel table with only a sheet covering him. He sat up. As his eyes adjusted to the dark he realised where he was. Pulling the sheet away he could see the label tied to one of his toes.

The weight of his realisation came to him in a rush bringing with it memories of almost twenty years before, something dark and secret which he thought he had cured himself of. Obviously not.

He rose and tore off the label, made his way to the door, carefully opening it. There was just one small light left on in here, a room full of shelves and boxes. The room was empty of staff, it must have been the middle of the night.

He soon found the box he searched for and took out his clothes. Dressing quickly although the shirt was useless, it was crimson with dried blood so he rooted through some other boxes until he found a pullover to fit. He then silently made his way outside the morgue undetected.

He couldn't go home, so where? He decided simply to get clear of the city first.

The his surprise his wallet and cash were still in his trouser pocket so he hailed a taxi and gave directions to a small hotel on the edge of the city, knocked up the night porter and got himself a room for the night.

The porter commented "You look all washed out mate, would you like something to eat, sandwich maybe?"

"No thanks, I just need some rest." He signed the register Jones, then made his way to his room, locked the door and lay down to think out what he was now to do. Now that Keith Stubbs was officially dead, who was he?

Chapter 18

RETREAT

※✦※

S TAN TYLER CAME out personally to pick Dan up. He tried to break the news of Keith Stubbs' death as gently as possible.

However he told it, Dan was devastated but seemed oddly relieved in his curiosity over the disappearance of his body. Dan was fairly sure the Count had not taken it as he had been in Tarporley all the time with Dan, but there was one other explanation although Dan could never voice his suspicion of it.

Back at Tyler's office the Police turned up and Dan gave his story as simply as he could.

He explained that Matthew Farnham had held him hostage while he sent Stubbs off with his two thugs to try to find his daughter, much more than that he did not know except he had woken up early this morning to find the house empty and could only presume that Farnham had heard of the killings and fled.

The police though not happy accepted Dan's story then sent a message to Cheshire Police to check out the house As expected it was empty and the estate agent who had rented it out had been paid well in advance but had no forwarding address for Matthew Farnham.

Two months later saw the completion of the sale of Dan's and Stubbs' house (at a greatly reduced price). Dan was not interested in the money, he simply wanted to get away somewhere quiet and try to come to terms with the dreams which were getting worse all the time.

Still in fear that he may turn at any time, for the first time ever he felt the Count had not told him enough and wanted his questions answered, but he was not likely to go looking for him for fear of what the Count may do next, especially if pursued.

With all outstanding affairs settled Dan said his goodbyes to Stan Tyler saying only that for now he was going to rent a cottage in the New Forest area and seek only peace and quiet for some time.

The dreams haunted Dan to the point where he tried constantly not to sleep. This only served to make his depression deepen.

Often his thoughts would wander to memories of Anna. A jumble of mixed emotions, sometimes blaming her for his seduction and consequences thereof. Sometimes blaming himself for not staying with her after the events at the castle. But always wondering where she may be now, agonising over the fact that the Count was searching for her, feeling useless in his ability to potentially defend her from her fate.

Then the ultimate admission that if he could find her and rekindle their love he may be no better for her than the Count. He had no release from his misery, waking or sleeping.

Chapter 19

LIFE IN THE FOREST

❧✦❧

D AY OR NIGHT made no difference to Dan. His senses keener
than ever, he walked constantly through the woodlands and
across the heaths surrounding his cottage.

People were beginning to grow accustomed to the bedraggled pale
beggar obviously once a big man but now old and stooped as if he had
given up on life itself.

He had deprived himself so long what he craved that his reasoning
and will to live were rapidly disappearing. He simply wandered from
town to town begging cups of tea or scraps and handouts since the
money he once had simply frittered away. He slept down in the
woods, washed in streams. In fact the only thing he put any effort in
was to resist his urge for warm human blood and its tender flesh.

It had taken nearly ten years last time to beat the cravings but life
had been a little easier then and the truth of his suspicions not so sure.

After twelve months Dan began to feel worse if that were possible.
He had begun to socialise a little in several of the quaint pubs about,
but recently the talk in them had been of something about killing and
mutilating livestock.

Stubbs woke, hungry, thirsty and cold. Something was wrong, he
sat up and thought. Everything was becoming cloudy. "I am . . . I am"

His brows knitted in confusion, he was getting frustrated at not being able to remember.

Trying to pull himself away from his despair he stood and ambled off through the woodland towards the Beaulieu river as he had spent that night in Hartford Copse. Dropping onto his hands and knees he drank deeply from the flowing water quenching his thirst. He had already lost all thoughts of his confusion over his identity. The quiet of dawn disturbed only by the waking chirps of birds and the bubbling tumbling sounds of the river.

He started as something broke though the brush behind him. Jumping sharply to his feet as he turned, realising it was only a mare with her foal coming to drink at the same spot, but at his reaction the mare turned her foal away, eyes blazing with fear at the sight of the bedraggled beggar.

The sight of the disappearing horses turned his mind to that of flesh and seeking out a way to sate his hunger. Walking briskly to warm himself he crossed the Beaulieu Road, crossed the heath and made his way into the deeper woodlands of the forest. He had given up begging for favours in the towns and villages around the forest months ago.

Stealing a chicken from one of the farms about had become something he was fairly adept at. so chicken in hand he settled in a patch of woods at Moon Hill intending to cook and eat his breakfast.

The sun was up when he woke again having eaten, but this time he did not remember building a fire to cook the chicken although he did remember eating it. He looked about and then knew there was no evidence of a fire. What puzzled him was he felt far more satisfied after eating one chicken than he ever had before. Then he realised he had eaten it raw, intestines and all.

Dan had heard of the beggar, not often seen these days in the towns and villages around the forest, but had never given him a second thought believing Stubbs to be dead.

He was despondent his life was empty but he had no heart in looking towards finding an occupation in which he could interest himself. He knew he would have to find work soon as the money from Stubbs' will and the sale of the house was rapidly diminishing.

Stan Tyler had offered him work any time he wanted it but Dan couldn't bring himself to take it on without the support of Keith Stubbs whose death he blamed himself for.

"The only man who ever really helped me out when I was in a tight spot" he was known to say with monotonous regularity.

On his walks in the woodlands Dan had got to know most of the rangers. It was with Dave Stockton, the Head Ranger, he walked with this particular overcast afternoon. Dave was preoccupied with disturbances at some of the local stables and kennels. Reports of the animals being more nervous than usual.

"I think we have probably got a stray dog on the loose or one somebody, a camper or tourist, has abandoned. None of the local kennels have reported any missing."

Dan Stockton rambled on getting his troubles off his chest but the more he talked the more Dan became intrigued.

Some badger sets had been uprooted and all the badgers mutilated but the thing that caught Dan's attention was when Stockton mentioned that in all the badger sets only the skulls were crushed and eyes and brains gone, presumably eaten by whatever animal killed them.

He was worried that it may be a rabid dog and asked Dan to treat what he told him in strict confidence.

Dan's curiosity was aroused. He had a feeling that there was a lot more to these happenings in the forest than any of the local people suspected.

Frightened of what he may find but feeling a confrontation with what was possibly the perpetrator of these mutilations he decided to track it down and face his nightmares head on, live or die.

Dan's senses were as sharp as ever but the forest was a big area to search for a single scent so he called Dave Stockton and asked him out for a drink intending to try to find out where the badger sets were disturbed.

They met in a pub in Brockenhurst, shared a few stories and drinks and eventually Dan got Stockton to admit where one of the uprooted badger sets were.

Dawn the next morning found Dan deep in the centre of Parkhill enclosure rummaging around the old badger set. Then he caught it, faint but definitely that of something he recognised, the scent of the wolf and the man. Part of it familiar but part not. He had expected to find a trace of the Count's scent, the scent of a turnskin. He had found one but it was not the Count's Then the realisation hit him, another werewolf.

"Oh!, my God, where will this end?" Dan wasn't sure what to think now. He even wondered if it could be him but although the dreams tormented his nights he still was unaware of any physical changes or turning.

Tracking the scent was fairly easy to Dan even though he knew it was a few days old and fading, washing away by the light rain beginning to fall.

It took him most of the day to reach the spot where whoever or whatever, he was tracking had spent the previous night. Dan checked the map he carried and surmised that he was in Hartford Copse.

The scent left here was strong but still puzzling him was the odd familiarity though he now definitely knew it was not the Count's smell he could detect.

Stuffing some of the crumpled brush into his coat pockets as a reminder of the spore he decided to call it a day and start afresh in the morning at first light and set off towards his rented cottage across the forest.

Knowing the possible danger of what he was doing, on his way home he tried to keep mostly to the heath rather than the wooded areas which meant it was after midnight by the time he got home.

Then it hit him, strong and fresh. Whatever it was he had followed all day had been here. The scent was strong and fresh. Dan let himself into his cottage and paced nervously up and down after double checking all the doors and windows were locked. He also took out the shotgun he kept in the cupboard under the stairs and loaded it.

It was only now he realised that all day he had no way of protecting himself whilst out in the woods.

He did not sleep that night.

A fine mist hung over the forest. It was just after dawn when Dan actually plucked up the courage to venture out. Taking no chances this time he cradled the shotgun in his arms.

The scent had faded slightly but it was not too difficult for Dan to follow.

After an hour Dan sensed he was getting close. Making his way through the copse he had tracked his quarry too. He picked up the sounds of what seemed a man sleeping deeply.

Dan's knuckles were turning white grasping the shotgun and his pulse raced as he peered through the bushes. The sight that struck his eyes almost caused him to faint. Reaching out to grab a nearby branch to steady himself the shot gun fell from his grasp onto the soft earth without Dan even realising it, as he stared open mouthed at his dead partner, Keith Stubbs. Four stone lighter and bedraggled like a vagrant, but without doubt it was Stubbs.

Chapter 20

REUNION

IT TOOK DAN fully fifteen minutes to wake Stubbs. He was fairly delirious as he came awake not recognising who Dan was.

"Who are you? Do I know you, why should you want to help me?"

Dan did not answer any of Stubbs' questions he just kept reassuring him that he was a friend here to help. Eventually he got the weakened wasted man to his feet and cradling him with his arm around his shoulder the two staggered off into the woods in the direction of Dan's cottage.

Once there Dan sat Stubbs on the couch and made some hot soup feeding it to the weakened man with some bread. No sooner had he finished his third bowl when he vomited it all straight back up over the floor of the cottage.

It was with some effort that Dan eventually managed to get Stubbs upstairs and after stripping his tattered clothes off, put him to bed. Shocked again when he saw the condition of his friend's scared body.

After Dan had cleaned up the cottage and made up another bed in the spare room he remembered he had left his shotgun in the forest.

Checking Stubbs was still fast asleep he hurried across the wood and searched for the shotgun. He gave up, impatient to get back to the cottage trying to think up an excuse for the loss of it should someone report finding it, eventually giving up and hoping nothing would come of it.

As soon as he arrived back at the cottage he checked on Stubbs who was still safely tucked up in bed, fast asleep.

He sat with a glass of brandy trying to remember all Stubbs had ever told him of himself which was not easy as he had kept a lot of doors locked about his life before they met.

After two days of nursing Stubbs, Dan found the only thing Stubbs could keep down was water and lightly cooked meat.

Although now he became coherent he admitted that there was something about Dan that he couldn't quite recall but it was there.

The more they talked (though it was more Dan talking and Stubbs listening than anything) the better Stubbs seemed to get.

Occasionally, Dan would have to stop Stubbs wandering off into the woods.

After about a month of this Stubbs seemed to be coming round to being more talkative, remembering snippets of things, mostly trivial. Then one evening he asked Dan "Who is the Count."

Dan was startled and thought instantly that this might be the way into the light. They sat up until after midnight while Dan related all that had happened in Poland.

Stubbs seemed to recognise some details but when he mentioned Eva something came over Stubbs and he went into a sort of trance, struggling to find his memories for a short time, then came out of it asking Dan to continue.

The next morning Dan called Stan Tyler. He gave him all the details he knew concerning Anna and Eva and asked him to try to contact them, without letting him know about Stubbs.

It was three weeks before he heard from Stan Tyler in which time Dan had been marginally successful in weening Stubbs off virtually raw meat and back towards a more normal diet. This action also seemed to help him from his almost unshakable stupors he would drift into most days.

Some nights Stubbs would try to leave the cottage but since Dan's dreams were still so disturbing to him he slept very lightly and always managed to wake and prevent Stubbs' nocturnal wanderings. Although it was now beginning to tell on Dan's health. He often despaired and would begin to wonder if it would not be better if they were both dead.

When Stan Tyler called and told Dan that the girls were on their way from Krakow to London, Dan brightened. The thought of seeing Anna again cheered him tremendously and filled him with hope that Eva may stir enough memories and emotion into Stubbs that they may get somewhere in trying to bring him back to his old self. At least Dan had managed to put a little weight back on him. He now weighed around thirteen stone.

When Stan Tyler knocked on Dan's door he almost fainted. Stubbs pulled open the door and stared blankly at him showing no recognition at all.

Fortunately Dan arrived quickly enough to calm him and hold him up by his arm although he had to push Stubbs out of the way to do so.

By this time Eva had learned pretty fluent English from Anna. She turned on the shaky man immediately. "You lying bastard, you told me Keith was dead."

Stan Tyler's only response was not directed at Eva though.

"I . . . I don't understand."

Dan sat Tyler down in a chair, dispassionately and hurriedly turned to the two women standing on his doorstep.

He embraced Anna first, lovingly and long, then turned giving Eva an affectionate hug before ushering them into the cottage.

Stan Tyler heard everything Dan told him with corroboration from Anna and Eva. He then went on to tell of their work for Stan and the return of the Count. Both of the women turned pale and frightened when they heard of the Count being alive.

Stan Tyler broke in. "Don't you worry, I'll send some of my best men down here as security if this—erm your brother, or father, whichever it is turns up. I'll arrange everything first thing tomorrow. The cottage next door is empty I will see if I can rent it and I may even spend the weekends here myself."

To Dan it seemed that Stan had accepted everything a little too easily to really believe everything true. Dan thought Tyler more likely to form his own opinions about what really happened but he could not deny the presence of Keith Stubbs, a dead man alive.

Stan had been drinking with them all evening so accepted Dan's offer of the couch for the night. Eva sat up most of the night nursing Stubbs as he slept restlessly, calming him in his more disturbed moments.

Dan and Anna approached a night together cautiously, memories of the past hanging heavy, but once in each other arms in a warm bed, tired they both quickly drifted off to sleep and for the first time in ages Dan slept a deep dreamless sleep.

Chapter 21

SOMETHING IN THE WOODS

❦

STAN TYLER HAD managed to secure the cottage next door and arrange for several of his detectives to stay a week at a time bringing their families or girl friends with them to make things still look ordinary.

Some were sceptical of what their boss had told them.

"Supernatural and frightening goings on, keep an open mind" Stan had told them all, but most thought, humour the old man, more like a week's holiday than an assignment.

Dave Stockton knocked on the cottage door and was shocked when Anna opened it.

"Oh! er, is Dan home please."

Anna invited him in just as Dan came into the lounge. Eva was sitting on the couch while Stubbs still slept.

"Hi, Dave, how are you?"

"Fine, Dan, no wonder we haven't seen much of you lately. I'm sorry to interrupt but I need to talk to you in private. Have you got a few minutes?"

Dan agreed and told Anna he was just popping out for a few minutes.

Dan put on his coat and left with Stockton and walked along the pathway towards the woods. Dave Stockton first told Dan of how he had prevented one of his Rangers from handing in his shotgun to the police. Fortunately, his name was embossed on the stock and Stockton had recognised it.

"What were you doing out in the woods with it and how in hell did you come to lose it?"

Dan's excuse to Stockton was close to the truth but not completely. He explained a noise had disturbed him in the cottage, he had gone out to investigate carrying the shotgun but when he found the begger he was stunned realising he was a long lost friend and in helping him home he had lost the gun."

"You should have told me, Dan." Stockton was friendly but firm. "I've got it in the car, I guess from the company you have you've been pretty well preoccupied."

"Somewhat Dave, I'm sorry for not getting in touch. You know how things can be."

What totally surprised Dan was when Stockton told him the killings and mutilations had got worse. Dan had thought Stubbs guilty for the demise of local livestock and woodland animals.

"A couple of campers have gone missing, the police are starting a search now. More animals have been mutilated in the same way as the badgers we saw. I just wondered if you have seen anything on your walks, but I guess with company you haven't been out quite so much."

"Listen, I can't explain now but if a tall grey haired distinguished man turns up, let me know straight away will you."

Stockton agreed but asked Dan if the detective agency he used to work for might not be more help.

"They are on it too Dave, let's just say for now I want to look after the ladies staying with me and everything helps."

They walked back to Stockton's car where Dan picked up his shotgun, thanked him, telling him they would get together for drink soon.

Dan walked back into the cottage grim faced.

"What is wrong?" Eva asked. Stubbs now sat next to her on the couch drinking coffee but still didn't seem to be listening.

"I think he's already here." Both ladies went quite then Anna asked.

"You mean Manfred?"

"I am afraid so Anna, but Stan Tyler's men will be here soon, we'll be OK." It was the least confident statement Dan had ever made, but he had to sound sure for their sake.

Stan Tyler's men, two of them, one Dan had known to say hello to, the other he had not met, turned up the next day with two young women in tow. They introduced themselves to Dan and company and set about installing a bell between the two cottages in case of emergency.

They caused a little upset by constantly parking their cars on the green opposite the row of cottages turning it into a muddy mess with the rain that had not abated for over a week now. After several local people complained and a visit from Dave Stockton they stopped parking there as it was supposed to be an access point to a walkers and bridle path through the woods.

Stockton had called on Dan to tell him that his enquiries had turned up someone answering the description he had given him had rented one of the big houses on the edge of Bealen Heath, but they had not questioned him as yet, for some reason the police seemed reticent to disturb him.

Dan spent a lot of time at night just staring out of the window into what seemed the pitch black of the forest night. Even to Dan's sharp eyes it seemed darker and more impenetrable than usual in the constant drizzling rain. But something itched at him occasionally he thought he saw just what he searched for then they would disappear. Two red orbs of hate and evil. The eyes of the werewolf.

On the third evening of Dan's nightly vigils there was a knock at the door. Dan and Anna were in the kitchen washing up. Stubbs and Eva sat together on the couch. Eva got up to answer the door for their twilight visitor at the same moment as Dan dried his hands and picked up the shotgun feeling his senses prickle.

Eva pulled open the door stepped back and screamed.

Stood in the doorway looking spectral with the lounge light searching the gloom of the rainy evening was Count Manfred Versipellis.

Dan levelled the shotgun at him. He did not try to come in he simply stood there straight faced. Every trace of the burns on his face and head had disappeared.

Stubbs sat still staring at the Count frowning as if trying to remember something lost.

"What do you want here?" Dan's voice trembled as he spoke.

"You know very well Mr Hunter, I have come to take my Anna with me. If you let her come I shall leave you in peace."

Anna stood out of sight in the kitchen too terrified to look upon her kin.

"She stays with me, Count, leave us alone." Dan's efforts were boosted when Stan Tyler's men came to the doorway pistols in hand, behind the Count.

"You heard him mister, go now or we bury you."

The Count did not even turn to the men behind him. Calmly he spoke looking only at Dan.

"If this be the only way, so be it."

With that he turned not giving Tyler's men a single glance and strode off into the rain.

The two men stepped inside and closed the door. For a time nobody spoke.

Anna came out of the kitchen her fear turning to sobs. Dan put down the shotgun and held her.

"I guess that's the guy who is the werewolf then" one of Tyler's detectives put in tactlessly turning Anna's sobs to a full blown cry.

Dan simply shot them a glance cold enough to show what he thought of that comment.

"Er, if you need us again just ring." The other detective put in and hustled his partner out of the door.

Only then did anyone notice the look of rage on Stubbs' face he was flushed crimson, his fists clenched tight, his teeth clenched with his lips curled back. Eva tried to calm him, but he just sat as if in a trance.

It was around midnight, everybody was up. After tonight's events nobody even bothered to try to sleep.

Then came the howling sending shivers down everybody's spine except it seemed for Keith Stubbs. He had not moved all night and with the onset of the howling his eyes seemed to glaze over in rage.

Eva had sat away from him as he was beginning to frighten her. She was not alone in her feelings either.

Dan stared out of the window. This time he had no trouble spotting the two bright red orbs. His hands trembled cradling the shotgun. Nobody said a work, they just waited to see what would happen next.

Suddenly Stubbs stood upright and strode to the door. He looked Dan in the eye and spoke softly but with an absolute firmness in his voice. "Do not follow me." With that he pulled open the door slamming it behind him.

Dan instantly pushed the bell to alarm Stan Tyler's men but by the time they got to Dan's door Stubbs was three quarters of the way across the green, ankle deep in mud.

Eva and Anna watched from the windows. Dan and Tyler's men were just starting forward when a huge shadow shot from cover of the trees knocking Stubbs onto the muddy ground.

There seemed an interminable pause as the three men watched, rooted to the spot.

Chapter 22

CONFRONTATION

᠅

T HE TANGLED MASS of bodies exploded from the rain
soaked mud with an ear splitting howl accompanied by an
indescribable yell, the like of which no human ear had heard and lived
to tell of save one.

In the moonlight it was difficult to pick out the figures beyond a
shadowy blur except for Dan's keen eyes. But what he saw turned his
legs to jelly stirring in him a repulsion and a fear the like of which
made his first encounter with the werewolf seem trivial.

The Count in the form of the giant silver wolf was hurled from
the pit of mud landing with a dull thud as the air was forced from its
lungs.

Stood where they had seen Stubbs go down was now an
apparition horrifying enough to still the blood of anything alive, man
or beast.

Standing upright like a man at close to seven feet tall with long
rangy but muscled arms ending in what started out as a man's hands
ending at the knuckles then curling into horrific savage claws like
those of a giant grizzly bear.

Its body was bare showing great tufts of dark hair almost all over
except for where the back and parts of the chest ere covered with
white scars.

But worst of all was the shoulders and head. Huge trapezius muscles met at a thick hairy neck supporting a head so grotesque Dan could not stare at it for more than a couple of seconds. The eyes were completely black, the centre of the face was that of a deformed snout looking almost as if it had been squashed back into its own face with the lower jaw overlapping the upper with great upward protruding canine fangs and virtually no lips oozing great globs of saliva as its breath wheezed raggedly from its body.

It moved forward with a strange slow but ground covering lope coming upon the werewolf just as it managed to get back to its feet.

As it lunged the werewolf leapt to one side but not quite quickly enough and those hideous claws tore deep into the flesh of its hind quarters.

The werewolf spun viciously and bit into the leg of the creature almost cutting right through the flesh and thigh bone.

Screaming wildly the creature brought its arm upwards to full height and smashed down with those powerful claws into the centre of the werewolf's back. With a resounding crack the wolf fell from its grasp on the ground lay into a heap. It lay on the floor its jaw dripping blood, it back broken almost in two separate pieces. It had totally lost control of its bodily functions.

The creature not satisfied thrust one of its claws into the flesh behind the werewolf's head and slashed at the underneath of its neck with the other, completely severing the head from its body then holding the head high above its own gruesome head let out another scream that almost stilled even the wind.

It turned and tossed the werewolf's head at the watching people and for a split second seemed to stare Dan right in the eye before limping off, leaving a trail of blood, into the thick brush of the woods. Nobody volunteered to follow.

Epilogue

AT DAWN THEY found Stubbs' body slumped against the cottage door. He had died from loss of blood from the gaping wound in his thigh.

They burnt what was left of the werewolf that night, sorrowfully adding Stubbs' body to the funeral pyre at Dan's insistence though he offered no explanation.

The last deed was to dispose of the bones and ashes. This they did at dawn burying them deep in the muddy ground behind Dan's cottage.

Then they all packed and moved out.

THE END